Gabriel Hawke Novels

Murder of Ravens

Mouse Trail Ends

Rattlesnake Brother

Chattering Blue Jay

D1452610

Fox Goes Hunting
A Gabriel Hawke Novel
Book 5

Paty Jager

Windtree Press
Hillsboro, OR

This is a work of fiction, Names, characters, places, and incidents either are the product of the author's imagination or are used fictitiously, and any resemblance to actual persons living or dead, business establishments, events, or locales, is entirely coincidental.

FOX GOES HUNTING

Contact Information: info@windtreepress.com

Windtree Press
Hillsboro, Oregon
http://windtreepress.com

Cover Art by Christina Keerins
CoveredbyCLKeerins

PUBLISHING HISTORY
Published in the United States of America

ISBN 978-1-952447-07-5

Special Acknowledgements

Special thanks go to my guide while I was in Iceland, Ragnar Hauksson. He not only explained things to me while I was there but answered my numerous emails after I arrived home and needed information from places I hadn't seen while in Iceland. Judy Melinek, M.D. CEO, Pathology Expert, Inc. for answering my questions about a body in a sulfurous boiling mud pool. And my fellow authors and beta-readers from around the world who helped me get my character's dialog realistic sounding.

Author Comments

I was lucky enough to go on a literary tour of Iceland last summer. My guide and fellow authors had a good time helping me discover a place where my character could find a body. On our last day, we visited the boiling mud pots at Krýsuvik and I knew I'd found my murder scene. From there it was a matter of finding a way to get Hawke to Iceland and I discovered the biannual SAR conference held in Iceland and made him one of the instructors. From there the story took place in my head and came out through my fingers onto the keyboard.

Chapter One

Standing in line behind other pre-conference participants for one of the largest Search and Rescue (SAR) conferences Gabriel Hawke had ever attended, he felt as if he'd been swallowed by a whale and was one of the hundred other fish trying to find balance inside the beast's belly.

"I should have never let the lieutenant talk me into this," he muttered under his breath.

"Your lieutenant. My group captain told me to get up here and learn more about what happens on the ground."

Hawke turned to the female voice and found a woman he'd guess to be in her forties. Her skin had seen a lot of sun, giving her a leathery appearance.

She held out her right hand. "Mayta Moore, RAAF Australia."

He grasped her hand and gave it a firm squeeze, which she returned. "Hawke, Oregon State Trooper, USA." He'd been told SAR members from around the world came to Iceland for their biennial conference. He hadn't expected there to be so many people and from such faraway places. And this was just the group who'd arrived two days early to participate in the pre-conference courses. One of which he was teaching.

"You work the air or the ground?" Mayta asked.

"Ground. Usually horseback or foot. You?" He walked forward as the line moved several feet.

"Air. RAAF, that's the Royal Australian Air Force." She said it as if he didn't have brains enough to be at the conference.

He nodded and concentrated on moving forward in the line.

"Hawke! Over here!" A young man in his twenties waved a hand in a come over here manner.

Since the man had called his name, Hawke nodded to the woman and headed to the table where the young man sat.

"How do you know me?" he asked.

"I'm in charge of registering all the speakers and instructors. We have your photo in the conference book." He held out a hand. "I'm Jón Einarsson. Just call me Nonni, everyone does."

"Ok, Nonni. This is the first time I've been to this conference or any this size. What do I need to do?"

"Have you checked into your hotel?" Nonni held a large manila envelope out to Hawke.

"Yes. I arrived this morning. I'm staying across the street at the Center Hotel. It may not be the conference hotel, but it's easier to get here, and I prefer a quieter place than where other attendees are staying."

The young man smiled. "I read all about you. You are Native American and a very good tracker. Because I am so excited you are here, my father, Einar Leifsson, the conference coordinator, said I could help you with your pre-conference course."

Another attendee walked up to the table. "Hello, Nonni. Do you have my packet ready?"

Hawke could tell by the way the man spoke he was British.

"One minute, Reggie. I'm just finishing up with Hawke." The young man smiled at the newcomer and turned his attention back to Hawke. "I would like to be the person you track for your course tomorrow. Will that work for you?"

Hawke nodded. "I was going to ask your father who he would suggest. Can we meet sometime this evening to go over my thoughts?"

"I would like that very much. What room are you staying in?"

"Three-fourteen."

"I'll come by when I finish here, unless you will be out?"

"I doubt I'll be doing anything other than sleeping." Hawke put the manila folder into his backpack and spun around, scanning the area for stairs to take him to the bottom floor of the Harpa.

"What type of course is that gentleman teaching?" the British man, Reggie, asked.

Hawke didn't wait for Nonni's explanation. Usually, the first thing he did after registering, was scout out the rooms in the building where the event would take place. But after the four hour flight, the layover in a busy airport, another six hours on a plane full of people, and now the crowd registering for the event, he was ready for some alone time. Not to mention sleep. How anyone could sleep on a plane, he'd never know.

He passed the elevator on his way to the stairs. The doors opened and more people poured out. Hawke hurried by and then took the stairs at a leisurely pace. He'd seemed to be hurrying from place to place since he'd left home. Savoring the feeling of relaxing, he breathed a sigh and hoped he'd make it through the next five days.

He grinned. After the conference, Dani was flying in to join him for a week. When he'd mentioned he was coming to Iceland, she'd said it was one place she'd not managed to hit while flying for the Air Force. The next thing he knew, she told him she'd purchased a ticket to arrive the day after his conference finished. And he'd better plan on staying a week to travel about the country with her. When he'd asked for two weeks of vacation, Sergeant Spruel's eyes bugged out and he'd started asking Hawke if he had a medical issue or if his mother had one.

In his sixteen years as a State Trooper, working as a Fish and Wildlife officer in Wallowa County, he'd only asked for two weeks off when his mom had a medical emergency. He preferred to take a couple days here and there rather than be off for so long.

He'd miss Dog, his horse, and mule, but they were being well taken care of by his landlords, Herb and Darlene.

Walking out into the overcast day, growing grayer with dusk, Hawke navigated across the four lane streets parallel to the Harpa and the harbor, and the other street turning in front of his hotel.

Stopping and facing the tall Harpa building, he

allowed the colored oval-shaped panels of glass to soothe his frazzled nerves. The building had given him energy two hours earlier when he'd stepped onto the sidewalk and dreaded registering. Now, knowing he wouldn't have to set foot in it again until tomorrow, he could drink in the calming aesthetic.

He entered the Center Hotel. The young woman behind the desk greeted him. "You are popular. I have three messages for you."

"Thanks." He took the messages and headed to the elevator to take him to his third-floor room. A room which overlooked the Harpa and harbor.

Inside his room, he slapped the packet Nonni had given him on the dresser and dropped onto the bed. The first message was from Sergeant Spruel wanting to know if he'd arrived. The second was from Darlene. Also wanting to know if he'd made it, and the third was from a person named Sigga, wanting to meet for drinks in the Bergmál bar in the Harpa at 8 PM tonight.

Uncertain who Sigga was, he put that one to the side and texted both his sergeant and his landlord that he was settled into his room and registered for the conference.

Drinks at 8. He glanced at his watch. He had three hours until then. A two-hour nap was in order.

Hawke stepped out of the elevator and into the lobby of his hotel as Nonni and three other people, also in their twenties, walked into the hotel.

"Hawke. I am here to visit with you." He waved to the young people following him. "These are Ásta, Bragi, and Katrín. My friends."

"Nice to meet you," Hawke said. He glanced at his

watch. "I had a message to meet with someone named Sigga at eight in the Bergmál bar at the Harpa."

They hid snickers at his pronunciation of the bar's name.

"Yes, she is a member of SAR. She will be your helper for your seminar." Nonni shrugged. "If you wish to speak with her, we can follow and talk with you when you and Sigga are finished."

It would be rude to not meet with this woman even though the young man made as if it wouldn't be a big deal to blow her off. He came here by request of his lieutenant to be a representative of the U.S. and to perhaps learn some new techniques from the Icelandic SAR members. He might as well deal with Sigga and then Nonni. That way they would all be ready to roll tomorrow for his class. "Come on along. If you know who she is, you can point her out to me."

The quartet of Icelandic young people chatted in both Icelandic and English as the five of them crossed the streets to the Harpa.

"Can you tell me, is this a conference center?" Hawke asked the young woman walking beside him. He believed Nonni said she was Katrín.

"A concert hall first, then conference center, and restaurants, also a place to purchase things." She smiled as he held the door open for her. "This is the gem of our city. The colored glass walls are a piece of art. What better place to have concerts and plays?"

Hawke had noticed the stores on the ground floor when he'd entered the building earlier. Now they were closed for the evening. Yet, there was still a lot of activity. Mostly on the second floor where he could see conference attendees were still arriving and registering.

He was glad he'd been early and it was behind him.

Nonni led the group under the open loft above and down a hall. The girls moved closer to the boys, and Hawke realized they were two couples out having a good time.

It had been a long time since he'd hung out with other couples his own age and enjoyed an evening. In fact, it hadn't happened since his divorce thirty years ago. After the destruction of his marriage, he'd stayed away from women, involvement, and having a good time. Until Dani Singer came into his life. He was crazy at his age to get hot and horny over a woman. But there it was. He'd fallen hard for the ex-Air Force pilot. So much so, she was meeting him here to spend a week together exploring Iceland.

He shook his head and followed the group of young people into a classy restaurant with a ground view of the harbor and businesses along the shoreline. The moon was out just enough to give an ethereal light over the boats, water, and buildings outside the wall of windows.

"Hawke, Sigga is over there," Nonni said, drawing his attention from the view and back to the room.

A tall, slender blonde sat at the bar beyond Nonni's pointer finger.

"We'll be over here when you are finished," the young man said, guiding his group to a small table near the wall of rectangular beveled glass.

Hawke walked over to the woman and held out his hand. "Hawke."

She glanced at his hand, then up at his face. "Sigga." She grasped his hand and drew him to the chair beside her. "Welcome to Iceland. I was told this is your first time to our country and this conference."

"It is. I like what I've seen so far of your country. I'm looking forward to seeing more tomorrow afternoon when we do the actual tracking." He motioned for the bartender. When the man arrived, he ordered a beer and another for the lady.

"Thank you," Sigga said, studying him. "Are all Native Americans as large as you are?"

He'd wondered about the curiosity of the Icelandic people to his culture. "Are all Viking women tall and thin?"

Her eyes narrowed. "I am Icelandic and can find ancestors who were offspring of the Vikings. However, Vikings were pirates who settled here from Norway."

"I'm sorry. It would be like you calling me a savage when I am an American Indian."

She nodded, but her eyes remained blank. "For some they would not wish to be called Viking, while there are others who boast of being descended from Vikings." She sipped her drink and returned her gaze on him. "I expected you to have longer hair."

"And moccasins?" he asked, taking a drink of his beer. He'd learned a long time ago not to get angry, to educate. In the military and even when at the State Police Academy, he'd dealt with misconceptions his whole life.

"No. I didn't expect you to come here wearing animal skins." She frowned. "Are you making fun of me for being curious?"

"Maybe, a little. My hair is short because of my occupation. Even if I were not in an occupation that required my hair to be short, I would keep it manageable. I believe in the Creator and how the land

14

belongs to us all and we should all be stewards of the land and the animals who live on it, but I rarely go to Powwows or join in any drumming or dancing. I'm too busy doing my job—keeping the animals and people safe in Wallowa County."

"Wow. I didn't expect to get a whole story from you." She sipped her drink and continued to stare at him.

Her scrutiny made him nervous.

"You asked me to meet you. What did you need to tell me that couldn't be done before my course tomorrow?"

"If you need photocopies made, I will do it. Have you planned where the tracking route will be and who you will track?" Sigga sipped her drink.

"I'm discussing that with Nonni when we're through. He offered to be tracked." Hawke glanced the direction of the young people who'd led him to the restaurant and bar.

Her gaze followed his. "That's Einar's boy. Are you sure you want him to know what's going on? He can't keep anything to himself." She frowned. "I could make it harder for you and the class to find me than that *sá aumingi.*"

Hawke studied the woman. "How are you connected to SAR?"

"I'm the Chief Inspector for Hvolsvöllur. It's a town in the mid-south of the country." She placed her empty glass on the bar and picked up the one Hawke bought for her. "I am usually in command of the search and rescue missions southeast of the Reykjanes Peninsula."

"The only person who will know where we will be

tracking besides myself is Nonni. That way no one can speculate ahead of time. Tracking is as spontaneous as it is methodical." He finished his drink. "I'll see you at my class tomorrow morning. I presume I can count on you to hook up my laptop to a screen for the class to view?"

"Yes. But I had hoped to help you with more than just technical support." Her gaze drifted from his face, to his crotch, and back up to his face.

Hawke shook his head and wandered over to Nonni's table.

Chapter Two

"Watch along the road and any off roads for the car matching the description I gave you." Hawke stood in the front of the bus, facing the thirty conference attendees who'd wanted to learn more of the hands-on tracking. He was happy to have this few. It would make splitting them up and not compromising any tracks easier.

He'd had a good discussion with Nonni the night before about the area he wanted the young man to "get lost" in. It was rugged, rocky, and would make finding tracks hard. His course was on tracking when there aren't any tracks.

They traveled along Highway 42, getting close to the area around Lake Kleifarvatn that he'd suggested Nonni roam around trying to leave a trail. The young man had left at nine that morning when Hawke started showing photos of areas that were hard to track in and how you had to use more than actual tracks to determine the direction a lost person might have gone.

Nonni knew to drive here and begin hiking. It was now 12:45. He would have had plenty of time to leave several miles of trail and have them all get out of here by dark.

"Are you sure this is where he will be?" Shiro Tanaka, a policeman from Japan, asked.

"I told him to drive this highway and pull over when he found a good spot." Hawke wasn't going to reveal he'd also asked him to park where there would be enough space for the bus.

"That helps," Páll, an Icelandic policeman, said, relaxing back against the seat. "This time of year there isn't a good place to pull off without getting stuck before the Krýsuvík mud pools parking lot."

Hawke glanced at the person. Now no one would look and work their investigative senses.

The bus chugged along and slowed at the site of a large parking lot. Beyond the parking lot, there were half a dozen colorful, steaming, pools of mud with walking paths and several wooden walkways. A few people, probably tourists, were already walking around, taking photos.

"Want me to drive in?" the driver asked.

"Yes. There aren't very many vehicles." Hawke had already spotted Nonni's car.

"There it is," Sigga said, as the bus turned into the parking lot.

"Pull up beside that blue sedan parked near the edge," he ordered the bus driver. Hawke faced the group. "Stay behind me and away from the vehicle while we discuss how to figure out which direction he's gone."

Hawke exited the vehicle first. A glance at the dark gray clouds and the sharp biting wind on his neck, had him pulling the collar of his coat up around his ears. He'd been wise to bring his felt Stetson in this weather. "Make sure you are all bundled up. Don't want to have any of you get frostbite." He walked over to within ten feet of the blue car.

The group gathered where he motioned for them to stop. "The first thing to do when you encounter the vehicle of a missing person is take a look around for prints to show you which way they are headed."

"This is paved. There are no footprints," said one of the attendees.

Hawke pulled plastic evidence markers from his backpack and crouched, studying the ground. "We know that he left Reykjavik at nine this morning. How long did it take us to drive here?"

"About forty minutes," Sigga said.

"Then we must figure that," Hawke glanced at his watch, "he arrived before the sun dried the dew from the ground, and we are four hours behind him." Hawke spotted something on the ground. He placed an evidence marker near it.

"What is that?" Kanika Tumaini, a policewoman from Kenya, asked.

"Something that isn't natural to this parking lot." Hawke explained why he thought the small pebbles that scratched the surface in a line were important to the tracking. They showed movement toward the path leading to the boiling mud pools. "Split up into groups of three and check along the paths to see where someone stepped off and headed away from this area."

He pointed to Ms. Moore, Mr. Tanaka, and Ms. Tumaini. "You three check out the vehicle and see if you can find anything that would tell us which direction he is headed."

"I've never searched a vehicle before," Ms. Tumaini said.

Hawke studied her a moment. "Just follow the other's lead. I'm sure you'll figure out what we need after you look." He didn't know if Nonni had left anything in the car to help the search. But it was a good lesson. You don't always find easy directions to follow.

A whistle and a shout went up. "Over here!"

Hawke jogged to the spot where Chelsea Pearce, a SAR from Colorado, Sigga, and Reggie Carlton stood.

"This looks like a clear hiking boot print that is headed east, toward the road and more open ground," Sigga said.

"And the sign says not to walk here," Chelsea pointed out.

Hawke studied the print. It was the correct size for the young man. He hadn't had a chance to see what his hiking boot soles looked like. "Good job. While we have been given permission to trek around out here, try to spread out a bit to not make too much of a mark on the landscape. You'll take turns in the lead." He glanced back at the three still at the car. "Would someone run back and get the people at the car?"

A thirtyish man from the U.S., Leonard Harlow, ran back.

Hawke pointed to one person. "You start following the trail. If you lose it for any reason, stop and ask for help. With this many people tramping around, the tracks could be wiped out by our feet if we aren't careful." This was not only a lesson on following sign but how to not cover it up.

They crossed the road and the lead person stopped at the other edge. "I lost it."

Hawke had known that would happen. "Everyone take a good look at what the boot print looks like." They each leaned over studying the print, then awaited his next command. "Now, spread out along both sides of the road and see where he stepped off the pavement."

While the group looked for tracks on the ground, Hawke studied the landscape. Knowing Nonni would be trying to outfox them, he looked for the terrain least likely to show prints. He spotted a rim of pillow lava about thirty yards to the east.

"Over here!" Ms. Moore called.

Hawke jogged over along with the rest of the group. There was a clear print in the mud alongside the road. "Since you found the track, you can follow it until you lose it."

The woman gave him a defiant glare before dropping her gaze to the ground and moving slowly forward.

"When you are tracking, you not only follow the clear evidence but also take a look at the surroundings." Hawke watched as half a dozen stopped and studied the terrain. "Where do you think this person is headed. Think like they would. If it's someone scared and alone, they would seek a way to see better. They would go to the highest spot or follow a mountain downhill to civilization. What if it is someone hiding? What would he do?"

"Try to hide his tracks," Ms. Pearce said.

"Then he would head for that patch of rock,"

Carlton said.

"Good thinking. Where is Ms. Moore headed?" Hawke asked.

Carlton smiled. "Toward the rocks."

At the small patch of pillow lava rock, the woman stopped, straightened, and turned a frustrated face his direction. "I don't see a track on the rocks."

"You couldn't have had much of a track to follow across that spongey grass. How did you know he came this way?" Hawke wasn't going to give anything away. He wanted them all to learn from this course, not just listen to him.

"Indentions in the grass and torn spots, like he was hurrying, maybe running or jogging."

"Good. That is the other thing to watch for. The way the prints look. It can tell you how fast or slow the person you are tracking is moving." Hawke crouched by the edge of the rocks where Ms. Moore had stopped. He was impressed with how the group had fanned out on both sides of her as she followed the prints. That way the prints weren't compromised.

Studying the rocks, he saw a loose piece had moved slightly, and not far beyond, a scrape from a rock, perhaps lodged in the tread of Nonni's shoe.

"Everyone get down like this and study the rocks. What do you see?" He waited for them to all crouch. "It isn't always about the print you have been following but how things are displaced."

"There, I see it!" Mr. Tanaka said, pointing to the scrape. "He went that direction across the rocks."

"Good. You take the lead for finding the track." Hawke stood and waited for the group to move forward, again spreading out.

Tanaka walked down a gully and up to the top of a small rise. There was more rock.

Hawke had to give Nonni credit, he'd worked hard at making the class think and study the ground.

"Let's see if someone else can pick up the trail." Hawke crouched to see which direction the young man had gone. He was headed more south now. It appeared toward another rise.

Ms. Tumaini pointed. "There. He's headed this way."

"Lead the way," Hawke said, impressed with the keen eyes of the group so far.

They crossed the rocks and walked over the slight rise.

A large, perhaps thirty feet long steamy, sulfuric smelling pool of mud could be seen bubbling at the bottom of the draw. Hawke stared at the pool. Something didn't look right. The group had continued on, following the footprints. He whistled and called, "Hey, has anyone looked around rather than just at the ground?"

The group stopped and stared at him. "What was one of the first things I told you about following tracks?"

"It's not always about the tracks," Tanaka said.

"That's right. Did any of you take a look around when we came to the rise?"

They all started scanning the area.

"Something is out of place at the pool," Sigga said. She started to head down the rise along with everyone else.

"Stop!" Hawke shouted, causing them all to halt. "Sigga and I will go check on the mud pool. The rest of you wait here."

He motioned for Sigga to follow him. Hawke went down the hill cautiously to make sure he didn't disrupt any evidence if what he saw at the pool was a body.

The closer they walked to the pool, he could see the legs and feet of a hiker. The upper body and head were face down in the steaming, boiling, muddy water. His nose twitched from the sulfuric gas that smelled like rotten eggs.

"*Fjandans*!" Sigga exclaimed as they stopped at the person's feet. "I would not wish this way to die on even my enemies."

Hawke agreed. He pulled out his phone and took photos, hoping it wasn't Nonni. He didn't have any idea what the young man was wearing. "Should we pull him out or wait for forensics?"

"The longer he is in there, the more deterioration. Pull him out. *Fjandans*! Do you think this is Nonni?"

"I hope not." A lump as sour and large as a lemon rolled around in his gut. He dug in his pack and pulled out latex gloves. The gloves had been to show the participants in his class what all they needed to have in their pack when they went out tracking. Now it was being used in a way he hadn't planned.

They each grabbed a booted foot and pulled. The mud made a bit of a sucking noise as the body was tugged from its grasp. They rolled the body over. The neck and hands were boggy and discolored greenish brown from the mud and minerals. The facial features, besides being greenish brown, were distorted and swollen.

"Do you think it's Nonni?" Sigga asked, again.

Hawke felt the body's pockets and found a wallet.

Inside was a soggy driver's license, showing this was indeed Jón Einarsson. Nonni.

"Shit!" He shoved the wallet back in the pocket and stared at the body. "Call it in and tell everyone to stay put up on the rise."

"This is my country, not yours. I'll give the orders." As she said this, she pulled out her phone and walked up the rise toward the group.

"How did you get in there, my friend?" Hawke asked, studying the area around the mud pool. Had he been standing at the edge looking at it and slipped? Hardly likely. The ground wasn't any rockier than what he'd hiked to get here. Had someone shoved him in? Or hit him on the head, knocking him into the pool? But why?

The young man seemed carefree and amiable. What could he have possibly been into that someone would follow him here and do this?

Sigga returned. "The CID are coming as well as Detective Inspector Ari **Böðvarsson**. This is his region." She glanced up at the group on the rise. "I didn't tell them who we found. But asked them to all write down what they remember from starting at the car."

"Good idea. It will keep them busy. How long until CID and the detective get here?" Hawke crouched next to the body, studying the ground. The Criminal Investigation Division would check the area for evidence, but he wanted to make sure anything that might get covered up by their arrival be tagged now.

"An hour." Sigga crouched. "What are you doing?"

He pulled out one of the evidence markers from his pack. "Looking for indentions that might indicate a struggle."

"You don't think he fell in on his own?" Her tone was noncommittal.

"Nope. He had help." He glanced up at the woman then back to scanning the ground. "What can you tell me about him?"

"His father has coordinated this event for the last ten years. Nonni has been helping him every year."

"Was he a SAR member?"

"Nonni? He was working his way up, but he was just a college student who helped with the convention and went out on a call or two. He didn't really have the drive to be more than a weekend member."

Hawke placed another evidence marker on the ground. "He and his father get along?"

Sigga stood. "There is no way Einar did this. He didn't see the sun for his son."

Hawke studied her. This sounded a lot like a comment his mother or an elder would make. "I'm assuming this means the father had strong emotions for his son?"

"Yes." Sigga faced him.

"But they have different last names. Wasn't Nonni his stepson?"

She stared at him. "In Iceland, the child uses their father's first name and adds either son or daughter. I am Sigga Eiríksdóttir, daughter of Eiríkur, my father. He is Eiríkur Egilsson, son of my grandfather, Egill Friðmarsson. That is why we usually call one another by our first name. It is less confusing."

Now he was understanding why the father and son had different last names. They had appeared to have the same bone structure and Hawke had thought that was just an Icelandic gene. "Then he will take this loss hard." Hawke always hated telling a parent their child had died. A murder was worse than an accident, however, both were world shattering to a parent.

"This could close down the conference." Sigga sighed. "I was having a good time getting to know the new people."

Hawke stared at her. "The conference attendees can't leave. They'll all need to be contacted about how they knew Nonni."

"We can't keep a thousand people here while we conduct a murder investigation. That could take months." She stared at him as if he'd had his bell rung too many times.

"We need to talk to his friends." Hawke placed another marker. "I'm going to follow these tracks. They aren't Nonni's boot tracks."

"Do we have to sit up on that hill all day?"

Hawke swung around to find Ms. Tumaini standing twenty feet from the body. She didn't glance at it, but kept her gaze on Sigga.

"You'll all need to be questioned," Hawke said.

"You know where to find us. Can't we take the bus back and attend another pre-conference event? We might as well learn something as sit up there watching you two." Ms. Tumaini waved an arm toward the group. "And it's cold just standing around."

"Take down the name of everyone on the bus and you may all go back to the conference. But don't say a word about this." Sigga stood with her arms crossed.

"Aren't they going to wonder about us coming back early?" The Kenyan stared back at Sigga.

"Just say something came up and we sent you back."

The dark woman was taller and broader shouldered than Sigga. She shrugged and headed back up the hill.

"I wonder why they made her the spokesperson?" Sigga questioned.

Hawke shrugged and followed the tracks leading away from the mud pool.

Chapter Three

Hawke arrived at the Krýsuvík parking lot as the bus pulled out and sleet started to fall. The group had made good time back to the bus. He'd lost the trail once over some boulders, but had managed to pick it back up. He could tell the person he'd followed had a long stride and had been hurrying. The footprint was of average size— a nine or ten for a male and ten or eleven for a woman. The problem with hiking boots— men's and women's were hard to tell apart. The weight could have been either a man or woman. A bit heavier than Sigga, but an average man, a husky woman, or someone lighter who carried a pack.

He studied the vehicles in the parking lot. Nonni's was still there. About a dozen people were walking on the trails around the sulfurous steaming mud pools. Five cars, besides Nonni's were in the parking lot. How did the murderer get away? Had he or she followed the victim here, parked, found the right place to kill him, then hiked back, got in their car, and drove off?

Out of habit, he walked through the parking lot, writing down the car licenses, makes, and models. Three were rental cars. After that, he shoved his hands into his pockets, put his head down and trekked the mile straight back to the lone mud pool where the body was found.

Topping the rise, he spotted a van, police car, and unmarked car on a nearly invisible road beyond the mud pool. Eight people milled around besides Sigga.

He walked up and stood alongside the policewoman.

"What did you find?" she asked.

"The person who did this hiked back to the parking lot." Hawke tapped his pack. "I wrote down the licenses, makes, and models of the cars there, but I have a feeling whoever did this is back in town acting as if nothing happened."

"You must be Hawke, the tracker Sigga and Einar have been talking about." A tall thin man held out his hand. "I'm Detective Inspector Ari Böðvarsson."

Hawke shook hands. "Pleased to meet you. Do you have enough pull to make sure no one from the conference leaves until they can each be excluded from the investigation?"

"Sigga was right. You are wanting to keep everyone here. Unless we have proof someone is involved in this, we can't detain them once the conference is over."

"Then you'll have to make sure we figure this out before the conference ends and don't let Einar's grief have him shorten it." Hawke didn't like having only five days, possibly six if the attendees in question stayed on for the Super Jeep Tour on Monday.

A woman dressed in white, carrying a clipboard, walked up to them. "I was told you have a photo of how the body was found?"

Hawke pulled out his phone and showed her all the photos he took.

"Send those to me." She handed him a card. "After seeing the photos, my preliminary response is to say this is a homicide. I'll know more after an autopsy to see if there was any blunt force trauma to the head or drugs involved."

"Thank you, Halla," the inspector said, dismissing the woman. He turned to Hawke and Sigga. "We won't know anymore until the autopsy."

"We need to talk to the people at the conference and Nonni's friends. The ones he was with last night. They were all at the table while we discussed where he would come today." Hawke wasn't going to wait around for the report. He had people to talk to and a short time to figure it out.

"I know who the three were. I'll dig up what I can find on them," Sigga said. "Give us a lift back to Reykjavik?" she asked the inspector.

He grunted and they trudged through the drizzle over to his car.

Hawke shook the sleet from his waterproof coat and Stetson before sliding into the back seat. Sigga took the passenger seat in the front.

The two in the front discussed how Einar would take the news while Hawke hunkered into his coat in the back seat, making a list in his mind of who he needed to talk to. Other than Sigga thinking the young man wasn't SAR material, she hadn't said anything bad about him. What would cause someone to follow him and push him to such a gruesome death?

The inspector parked at the Harpa. "You coming in?" he asked Hawke.

"Yeah. I want to be there when you tell Einar about his son." Hawke stepped out of the vehicle. The bus that had taken them to the mud pools stood beside the building. "Did you instruct the others not to say a word about what we'd found?"

Sigga nodded. "But you know how people are. I would bet at least a third of them couldn't wait to get back and say they found a body."

"But did any of them know who we found?" Hawke wanted to see the conference coordinator's reaction. He doubted the man had killed his son, but if there had been a grievance between his son and someone, it was sure to come out.

"The only person who was close enough to see would have been Kanika, but the face was unrecognizable so I doubt she would know." Sigga strode into the building alongside Hawke.

The inspector was two strides ahead of them. He walked up the stairs rather than taking the elevator and went straight to the room that had a handwritten sign that said "Base of Operations."

Once inside the door, they all stopped. Hawke had only met Einar once, briefly. It was when he had visited a U.S. SAR conference Hawke had attended.

Böðvarsson pointed to a man in the back of the room drinking from a mug and listening to the Icelander, Páll, who had been on the trip.

From the look on the coordinator's face, he appeared interested but not upset. He turned to the three of them. His eyes widened a moment before he held out a hand to Böðvarsson. "Ari, from what Páll has told me, I doubt you will have any witnesses to the body the excursion found."

"Can we go someplace else and talk?" Böðvarsson asked.

Einar's eyes narrowed. "Why?"

"I would like to keep this as quiet as possible." The inspector put a hand on the conference coordinator's arm and led him to a door at the back of the room.

Hawke and Sigga followed. The room was set up for a class, but was empty today.

"I don't understand. What has the body in the mud pool have to do with this conference, other than Hawke's class finding it?" Einar faced all three of them.

"The body was Nonni," Böðvarsson said it softly.

Einar stared at the three of them. His gaze lingering on Sigga. His mouth opened, then shut, then he rubbed a hand across his eyes. "No. You have to be mistaken. He wasn't police or SAR material, but he wasn't that clumsy." The man took a step toward Hawke. "He wanted to help you because he thought it would be a research opportunity. He wanted to be a writer of crime fiction."

"Can you think of anyone who would want to hurt your son?" Hawke asked. He was antsy to start talking to people. They didn't have a lot of time to get to the bottom of this murder.

"Hurt him? This was murder?" Disbelief widened the man's eyes.

"We won't know for sure until the autopsy is

performed, but Halla doesn't think it was an accident."
Böðvarsson motioned to a chair.

Einar shook his head. "Nonni got along with
everyone. You can ask his friends. The people here."
He ran his hands over his face. "How do I tell his
mother? And Ásta? They were talking about getting
married."

"For now, we need to keep the fact it wasn't an
accident quiet and bring in officers to take down
information of the whereabouts of everyone involved
with the conference; workers and attendees." Hawke
held Böðvarsson's gaze. He knew he was overstepping
giving orders when he had no jurisdiction in this
country, but he felt responsible for what happened to
Nonni. "Just have the officers ask everyone when was
the last time they saw Nonni, and if they'd had a
conversation, what it was about."

"Want me to call your co-chair to come take over
while you go home to your wife?" Sigga asked.

Einar nodded his head. "Yes. Please call **Börkur**.
Tell him he's in charge for the rest of the conference. I
don't think I can." The man bit his bottom lip. "Sigga,
will you walk with me out to my car?"

When the woman started toward the main door, he
stopped her. "I want to go out through the back doors. I
don't want to talk to anyone."

She nodded and they disappeared.

Böðvarsson was on the phone requesting as many
officers as could be spared to the Harpa.

Hawke walked to the table in the front of the room.
"I'd like to question the people who were in the bus and
then Nonni's friends."

The inspector nodded. "I'll have Sigga round up

the people who took your class. Who are the friends?"

"I only know their first names. Ásta, Katrín, and Bragi. Those are the three he was with last night when we discussed what he would do today."

"I'll find out their last names." The inspector shook his head. "We have very few homicides in Iceland. I'll be the first to say, while we know how to handle it, it's helpful to have you assisting."

"I'm assisting because I feel responsible for the young man's death. He wouldn't have been out there alone, if I hadn't sent him." Hawke could rationalize all he wanted that the young man had offered to be tracked and at the time, he'd had no problem sending someone out in country they knew, to be tracked. Now in hindsight, he wished he'd sent two people, but that would have made the tracking too easy.

"From what I understand Nonni offered. You didn't know he would come to harm." Böðvarsson walked to the door. "I'll go find Sigga."

Hawke nodded and pulled a notebook and pen out of his pack. He took off his coat and hung it over the back of the chair. What he wouldn't give for a strong cup of coffee.

Chapter Four

Sigga had rounded up all twenty-nine of the people who had been on the bus, including the bus driver. Hawke had to admit she was thorough.

The room was large. As each person came in, he advised them to sit up in the last row by the door. He didn't want the others to hear what he asked each person or their answers.

Sigga arrived with two large cups of steaming liquid. "Thought you might like some coffee."

"Thanks. I was wishing I had a cup when I started writing down my questions." He glanced up at the people fidgeting and whispering amongst themselves. "Are you sitting in with me or questioning other people?"

"I thought I'd give you my statement then go help with the volunteers." She sat across the table from him.

He nodded. "Did you see Nonni this morning?"

She shook her head. "The last time I saw him was last night when you were talking with him. I left after finishing my drink."

Hawke wrote that down. "And can you think of anyone who would want the young man dead?"

"I've been thinking about that ever since we discovered it was him. Honestly, he was likeable, happy to please, and made friends. I can't think of any reason a person would want to kill him."

He tapped his pen on the pad. "Do you think he came across someone crazy who killed him for no reason?"

Sigga studied the table in front of her for several seconds. "That's a possibility, but if the person walked back to the parking lot straight away and didn't leave any tracks that looked like they were confused or uncertain, I think that scenario can be ruled out."

Hawke let out a frustrated sigh. "Yeah. I thought the same thing. But figured I should run it by someone who lives here." He glanced at the group at the back of the room. "Send one of them over. Good luck with your questioning."

She nodded and stopped briefly at the back of the room before walking out the door.

Reggie Carlton walked up to the table. "Figured I might as well start this off."

Hawke motioned to the chair across from him. "When was the last time you saw Nonni?"

The man's eyes widened. "Is that who you found? Bollocks! How is Einar taking it?"

"As you might imagine. When was the last time you saw the young man?" Hawke wasn't going to get distracted.

"Yesterday. When he checked me in, right behind you." Carlton studied him. "Is that what he was talking about, helping you? Is he who we were tracking?"

"I'll ask the questions. How well did you know him?"

The man leaned back, staring at Hawke. "This has to frost your arse knowing he volunteered to be tracked and him ending up the way he did."

"How well did you know him?" Hawke stared back.

"This is my third trip to this conference. Nonni has been at every one of them. He helped, like yesterday, registering the speakers and instructors. He also did some troubleshooting of tech problems and kept family members busy."

"Family members? Of who?" Hawke wasn't sure what the man meant.

"Some of the attendees bring their families, turn the whole thing into a family holiday. Nonni usually guided sightseeing trips during the day for the family members while their spouse or parent was in classes." Carlton motioned to the group behind him. "Several of the group in here brought families two years ago."

"Did you ever hear how the sightseeing went?" They had gone astray of his line of questioning with the first person he questioned. But it never hurt to learn everything he could.

"Everyone always had a good time from what I'd heard."

"Ever hear anyone saying anything bad about him?" Hawke watched the man closely. He didn't flinch.

"Never."

"Who did you sit beside on the bus?" Hawke asked.

"Shiro Tanaka."

"Thank you. You can send someone else down."

Carlton nodded and stood.

"Don't tell anyone who the victim was."

"I take that to mean you are considering this a murder even if the questions hadn't already told me that." Carlton smirked.

"Until the autopsy says something different."

The man pivoted and walked to the back of the room. He pointed with a thumb over his shoulder and a person stood.

Carlton exited. A woman walked down the aisle and up to the table.

Hawke interviewed six more participants. None had seen Nonni or knew who he was. It was their first time at the conference, like Hawke, and they knew very little other than the trip on the bus, the tracking, and finding the body.

Chelsea Pearce sat across from him.

"Is this your first time to this conference?" Hawke asked.

"Yes. My boss came two years ago and said this would be good for me to attend." She looked annoyed. "Will this take much longer? I want to get rested for the climbing trip tomorrow."

"A person has died. Did you meet Nonni, the young man who was registering speakers and instructors?" Hawke studied the woman who seemed to care more about missing a class than helping find a killer.

She smiled. "The good-looking guy at the smaller

table?"

"Yes, that guy."

"I stopped by and chatted with him for a few minutes before someone walked up to the table. And I saw him this morning when I was eating breakfast at the hotel."

"Which hotel?"

"The Hotel Marina."

"Did you talk to him?"

"No. He was sitting in a corner with a young woman. They looked like they were deep in conversation." She glanced over her shoulder. "Can I go now?"

"Can you describe the woman to me?" Hawke needed to know who it was and if Nonni had mentioned where he was going to her.

"She was his age, maybe a little younger. Dark hair, Asian features. Pretty." She stood. "I really need to go."

"Who did you sit with on the bus?"

"Sigga."

He waved for her to go. "Send someone down."

Five more knew nothing that helped him.

Mayta, the Australian pilot, strolled up to the table. "Bet you didn't think you'd be runnin a murder investigation when you signed up for this conference."

He shook his head. "I'm not running the investigation. I'm helping. When we talked before, I had the impression this is your first time at the conference?"

"Yep, it is."

"Did you happen to meet the victim, Nonni?" Hawke went on to reveal how the young man had been helping register people the day before.

"Oh, the dag who called you over to the other line yesterday?"

"Dag?" Hawke questioned.

"Nerd, geek. He looked out of place here." She smiled.

"I see. He was the person we were following." Hawke studied the woman. Her eyes widened briefly before she leaned back in the chair.

"Then I guess he wasn't such a dag."

"Did you see him any time other than when you registered?" Hawke was still trying to figure out the woman. She seemed tough like Dani, but she hadn't shown the compassion he'd witnessed in his friend.

"No."

"Who did you sit with on the bus?"

"Leonard, from the U.S. He was too chatty. I sat with someone else on the way back. Didn't get her name." Mayta grinned. "We didn't talk."

"Thanks, send the next person." Hawke jotted down what little the woman told him and watched as the next person walk toward him.

Eight more people had nothing to tell him other than who they sat by on the bus.

Kanika Tumaini, the woman from Africa, walked up to the table.

"Have a seat, Ms. Tumaini."

"Kanika, please," she said, sitting and studying him.

"I'm surprised you weren't one of the first to come talk to me, since you wanted to get back here so badly to go to other workshops."

She didn't bat an eye. "It wasn't the workshops so

much as the cold. We do not have this biting wind and sleet in Kenya. At least not in the lowlands. I wanted to get where I was warm and dry. The bus and sitting in here, my toes are finally warming up."

He leaned back and glanced at her hiking boots under the table. "Don't you have on wool socks?" The boots looked adequate for keeping her feet warm and dry in the small amount of weather they'd endured.

"No, I did not think there would be this cold of weather."

He dismissed her feet and asked the same questions he'd asked all the others.

"No, I do not believe I spoke to the man. I sat with Mari on the way to the parking lot. I don't know who the person was I sat with on the way back."

She didn't look at him when she commented on the ride back. He figured she was too cold to remember much about the ride other than trying to warm up.

"Is this your first time to this conference?" he asked.

She hesitated, staring him in the eyes. "Yes."

"Thank you."

The woman walked slowly to the back of the room. He wondered at her ability to work a search and rescue as anyone other than a person at the base of operations. If just following the trail, they'd walked for only a mile, had made her that tired and cold, she shouldn't go out on any other outdoor workshops.

Five more people had no answers for him. They hadn't talked to or seen Nonni when they registered or any time before the workshop started and setting out in the bus.

Shiro Tanaka walked up to the table. "Mr. Hawke,

I was looking forward to your workshop. I am so sad it has ended in such a way."

"Thank you, Mr. Tanaka." Hawke motioned for the wiry man in his fifties to take a seat. "Have you been to this conference before?"

"Yes, I have come the last two times." He nodded his head.

"Are you acquainted with Reggie Carlton?"

"Yes, he is a good friend. We both brought our families with us last time." Tanaka's smile spread from one ear to the other. "My family much enjoyed the activities. My daughter, she come with me again, she like it so well."

"What's her name?" Hawke wanted to have a word with the young woman.

"Riku. Would you like me to bring her for you to meet?"

"When I'm finished, I would like to visit with her. What is your phone number?"

The man recited his cell phone number.

"Thank you. Since you have been here before you must have known Nonni, the coordinator's son?"

"Known? He is taking my daughter and others to a restaurant tonight." He smiled, nodding his head.

Hawke wasn't sure how to break the news to the man other than just blurt it out. "I'm sorry, but Nonni won't be taking anyone anywhere. He was the body we found."

The man's hand covered his mouth and his eyes grew round. "No! Not Nonni. He was good boy. Everyone like him."

"Someone didn't like him."

The man's expression shifted from disbelief to

thoughtful. "He was killed, not an accident?"

"At the moment we are treating it as a homicide. Can you think of anyone who had a grudge against him?" Hawke didn't want it to turn out that someone taking in the conference did the young man in, but it was strange that if someone from here had wanted Nonni dead, why did they wait until now? Especially, when there were law enforcement people from all over the world here who would be digging into the crime.

Tanaka shook his head. "It must have been someone crazy he came across. I never hear anyone say anything bad about him. He made the conference bearable for family members."

"Who were you sitting with on the bus?" While he had Carlton marked down, it didn't hurt to cross check.

"Reggie. We were talking about how much fun our families had last conference." The man wiped a hand across his eyes. "This is most distressing."

"I'll give you a call when I have time to talk to your daughter."

The man stood. "I am sure she will want to help you in any way. She did meet some of his friends the last time we were here."

More good news. "Thank you."

Tanaka seemed to have a little less spring in his step. It was clear the young man he'd found in the mud pool had made an impact on many people who had been at this conference before.

Chapter Five

There were only three people left at the back of the room. Leonard, Páll, and the bus driver. Hawke picked up his coffee cup and tipped it all the way. Nothing. He could use another cup and something to stop his growling stomach.

Leonard walked to the table and sat down as only a young man in his late 20s early 30s could do. His spine seemed to be made of wet pasta and his arms crossed across his chest. His vibe was uninterested and annoyed.

"I can't believe you have kept us waiting here for hours. Couldn't you have just called and asked us to come down here when you were ready for us?"

"Full name please," Hawke wasn't going to explain anything to the young man. It was obvious he'd not been part of an investigation before.

"Leonard Harlow. Which you should know by the

fact I signed up for your lousy workshop. I thought we were going to learn something. All we did was walk through the cold following other people and then stopped when you came across a body. You could have at least let us all have a look and see what we could deduce."

Hawke stared at the man. "The area couldn't be compromised by all your footprints." What he wanted to say; If you had been paying attention, we explained everything as we discovered the unseen trail.

"Is this your first time to this conference?" Hawke studied the man. His actions were defiant.

"No. I came four years ago with my dad. He's the sheriff back home."

"Which is where?"

"Montana. Medicine Lake."

"You said you were here four years ago. As a participant or a family member?" He wondered if Leonard had caught up with Nonni, who seemed to have had such an impact on the family members.

"Family member. I hadn't decided what direction I wanted to go yet."

Hawke didn't say anything.

"I decided to follow in the old man's footsteps. I'm a deputy now, and he wants me to take over the Search and Rescue program."

"Do you remember a person named Nonni when you were here before?"

The young man grinned. "Sure! He was a lot of fun. I saw him yesterday. We laughed about some trouble we got into when I was here. I hope to look him up tonight."

"That won't be possible." Hawke had always hated

telling loved ones a family member had died. He was
finding telling all these people who had fond memories
of Nonni about his death just as hard. "He was the body
we found in the mud pool."

"No way!" Leonard shot to his feet, walked a
couple of steps, and came back. He stared down at
Hawke with a lost expression. "That…the body half
in…" His Adam's apple bobbed.

"Can you think of anyone who would have wanted
him dead?" The best thing to do was push on. If
Leonard was going to become a deputy, he'd need to
learn to control his emotions and dig up the facts.

"No one. He got along with everyone. The younger
kids and the old people. He was one of those people
who knew how to blend in wherever he was." Leonard
dropped back into the chair. "Shit."

"Other than the trouble you two found four years
ago, did he talk about anything else? A person he
planned to meet or trouble he might be in now?" Hawke
was grasping.

"He said he was meeting his friends and talking to
you."

"So, you saw him before eight last night?" The
group had met him in the hotel lobby a little before
eight.

"Yeah, it was closer to six. I registered and then
went over and visited with him until someone came up
to his table. Then I went to my hotel and had dinner."

"What hotel?"

"Hotel Marina."

"Did you see him in the restaurant this morning?"
He wondered at the meeting with the young woman. So
far no one else staying at the hotel had seen him, other

than Chelsea.

"At the hotel? No. But I was running late. I met up with a girl last night and… I had trouble convincing her she needed to leave my room so I could make it to your class."

Hawke studied the man. "You picked up an Icelandic prostitute last night?"

Leonard's face reddened. "No! In this country, everyone sleeps around. It has nothing to do with if you like them or not. It's just, what they do." He grinned. "My dad said it was kind of like the free love movement in the states in the sixties and seventies."

He tucked that information away and asked, "Who did you sit with on the bus?"

"The pilot from Australia. She is one tight-lipped woman." He laughed. "Maybe she should go out and get laid."

"You can go." Hawke shifted in his chair. His butt was numb, his cup was empty, and his patience was wearing thin.

Páll walked up to the table. "I do not know how any of us could know anything about a body found in a *hver,* hot spring." He sat with his feet flat on the floor and his spine against the back of the chair. A one hundred percent difference from the last person who sat there. He was also a good fifteen, possibly twenty years older.

Hawke flipped a page in his notebook. "What is your full name?"

"Páll Gizuarsson."

"Is this your first time at the conference?"

The man smiled. "No. I have been attending the conference since the first year. It is my homeland, and I

48

have been with Search and Rescue since I became a police officer."

"Then you knew Nonni, Einar's son?"

The man's brow wrinkled. "Yes? What does this have to do with the body…" He sucked in air. "I see. Was that poor Nonni in the *hver*?"

"Yes. Do you remember when the last time was that you saw him?"

The man sat still, his eyes half closed as if he were using the backs of his lids as a screen to replay the last time he saw the young man. His eyes opened. "As a local, I volunteer at the event. I have talked with Nonni every day for a week, and did so yesterday evening as we were closing the registration tables for the night."

"Did he seem distracted?"

"No. He was excited. He said you and he were getting together. Ever since your workshop was scheduled, he'd talked of nothing but helping you." The man's eyes widened. "Was he who we were tracking?"

Hawke nodded.

"Poor boy."

"Can you think of anyone who would want to cause him harm? Or anyone he might have told that he was our subject to track today?"

Páll shook his head. "Everyone liked Nonni. What are the families going to do without him to show them around? He was a big help with that."

"Do you think he told anyone where he was going this morning?" Hawke asked again.

"If you told him not to, I am for sure he did not tell a soul. He was one to do as he was told."

"Who did you sit by on the bus?" Hawke was getting a picture of a young man who had no reason to

49

be killed. Yet, he had been.

"Ragnar Helgason."

Hawke noted the other man had said he sat with Páll.

"Thank you. If you can think of anything, let myself, Sigga, or Inspector Böðvarsson know."

The man nodded. Páll walked to the door, and the bus driver shuffled down to the table.

"Thank you for waiting so long," Hawke said, indicating the chair across from him.

"I get paid until I clock out." The man, in his forties, leaned back in the chair, his legs out in front of him. He had the air of someone who'd been questioned by the law before.

"Your full name please."

"Daniel York."

Hawke had thought the man sounded like an American, but he'd also said the local words with ease. "How long have you lived in Iceland?"

"Twenty years, give or take."

"Is this your first time helping out with the conference?"

"Yeah. The company I usually work for was contracted to help."

"Does that mean you don't know anyone connected to the conference?"

The man smiled. "This is an island with a small population. Half the Icelanders on the bus, I've toted somewhere. A couple of the 'bosses' I've seen in the bars."

"Did you happen to know Jón Einarsson, Nonni?"

The man stared at him. "His car was in the parking lot. It's the one you were interested in. Is he missing?"

The corners of the man's mouth twitched as if he were hiding a smile.

"He's dead."

The man didn't flinch. "They going to shut this circus down? I need this job. My wife is pregnant."

"How did you know Nonni?" Hawke had an inky feeling about the man. He was too casual, too uninterested.

"Met him a time or two at the bars. Nightlife is what Icelanders live for. Otherwise the winters can drive you crazy."

"It's not winter now." This was the first person Hawke had questioned that his radar said he might be involved.

"Getting damn close." York stared at him.

"The person before you—"

"Páll. Good guy," York interjected and smiled.

The man was trying to take the conversation away from Hawke. "Yes. Páll. You know him in an official capacity?"

"Oh sure, because he's a cop, you think I'd know him." The man scowled.

Skipping that line of questioning, Hawke decided to see if what Leonard said was true. "One of the people I interviewed said the unattached population here hooks up. Do you know if the girl Ásta that I saw with Nonni is a hook up or a girlfriend?"

"I would say they are good friends. From what I've seen, they have been pretty steady, so I doubt they are hooking up with anyone else." He winked. "I can get you hooked up tonight."

"I'm investigating a death, not here for a good time." Hawke wanted to finish questioning this man and get something to eat. "Did the same number of people ride to the mud pools as rode back on the bus?"

York scowled. "I'm not a damn teacher. It was your responsibility Teach, to keep track of the students, not mine."

"Fair enough." Hawke leaned back in his chair. "Can you think of anyone who would have wanted Nonni dead?"

"Honestly, no. He liked to party, but who doesn't? He didn't get into fights and knew how to talk his way out of sticky situations. He was a good guy. He's going to be missed."

"Thanks. You can go."

Hawke closed his notebook and stood. The last half hour the chair had numbed his ass. He shoved his notebook into his pack and followed York to the door. He needed food and to connect with Sigga and Böðvarsson.

Chapter Six

After catching a meal of lamb and a salad mix at the Bergmál, Hawke went in search of Sigga and the inspector. They were in the conference base room, comparing notes.

"We wondered if you had finished your questioning," Sigga said.

"I did and grabbed something to eat." Hawke slapped his notebook down on the table. "By all accounts, there was no reason for someone to kill Nonni. Everyone liked him."

The two officers nodded.

"He was an asset to this conference," Sigga said.

Hawke studied her. That was different than her description of the young man last night when he'd mentioned Nonni would be the person they tracked.

Böðvarsson nodded.

"Which makes me think, either he had a side only a

few people knew about or it was a random killing." Hawke assessed the two as they let his comment sink in.

The inspector shook his head and Sigga nodded.

"I don't think either scenario works with this death," Böðvarsson said.

Sigga glanced at the inspector. "A random killing doesn't make sense given what we know about the crime scene, but it makes more sense than anything else about why he was killed."

"We'll have autopsy results in the morning. Let's meet here at nine and decide what to do from there." Böðvarsson shoved to his feet. "I'm going to visit with Einar. Maybe he knows if something different had been happening in Nonni's life. He should be over the shock by now."

Hawke nodded. "I'm going to speak to Nonni's friends."

"Want me to come with you?" Sigga asked.

"No. I think they will be more open with me. I can't arrest them for anything."

"He has a point," Böðvarsson agreed. "He has no jurisdiction in Iceland. He is only helping us gather evidence."

Sigga appeared put out by the inspector's agreement.

Hawke held up his notebook. "Do you want copies of my questioning? And I'd like to see yours."

Böðvarsson grabbed the notebook. "I'll have someone type these up and tomorrow morning we will all have copies of our questioning."

Not having his notebook to study overnight, didn't set well with Hawke, but the others did need copies. "I could have someone at the hotel make photocopies of my notes and bring them to you in the morning." He put his hand on the notebook to take it back from the inspector.

"You do not trust me?"

"I trust you. I want to be able to read through it tonight."

The inspector released the notebook. "Very well. But you will need to bring copies in the morning or I will take the book. We need that information to complete the investigation."

"I agree." Hawke shoved the notebook into his pack and pivoted.

"Do you know how to contact Nonni's friends?" Sigga asked.

"I do." He glanced over his shoulder and held back a smile at her disappointment. Striding to the door, he left the room and found a quiet place to make a phone call.

"Hello?" a suspicious Mr. Tanaka questioned.

"Mr. Tanaka, this is Hawke. I was wondering if I could meet with your daughter now?"

"Oooo, yes. She is at Slippbarinn with friends. I will let her know to stay there and wait for you."

"Where is Slippbarinn?" Hawke asked.

"It is the bar on the ground floor of our hotel. Hotel Marina." Tanaka's voice held suspicion. "You do not know of this place?"

"I'm staying at the hotel across the street from the convention." Hawke wondered now at his need to be away from the other attendees. It was putting him at a disadvantage for knowing things about the conference and area.

"I see. She will be wearing red jacket and boots." The man ended the conversation.

Hawke stood out on the street. He had no idea which direction to go. Putting Hotel Marina into maps on his phone, he discovered he was less than half a mile from the hotel. Rather than finding a ride, he pulled the collar of his coat up and started walking. One thing he could do without in Iceland was the constant cold wind. He wished he'd brought a stocking cap. Even though it was dark and cold, a consistent trickle of people passed him as he walked to the hotel. Many were locals. He could tell by how they dressed in boots, scarves, gloves, hats, and warm coats. The tourists stuck out, like him, with inadequate outerwear.

Hawke found the street side entrance to the bar and walked in. The music was loud, people's voices hung just below the decibels of the band. Some areas were well lit, others dusky dens of people talking in one another's ears, and excited laughter.

With no clue how to find Riku in this packed establishment with uneven lighting, he walked up to the bar and waited for the young woman with dark hair to finish giving a patron a show of mixing his drink.

The woman sauntered down to his spot. "Hello. What would you like me to make for you?"

"A beer. Nothing fancy. Just a plain beer."

Disappointment crossed her face before being replaced with a smile. "That is easy."

While she busied herself at the taps, Hawke studied the few tables he could see. He didn't see a young Asian woman wearing red.

"For you," the bartender said.

He put some bills on the counter. "Take what the drink is and whatever your tip would be." The money here was hard to figure out. Everything cost thousands of krona. He hadn't taken the time to figure out the exchange rate and hoped everyone he placed money in front of was honest.

"You haven't happened to see a young Asian woman in a red jacket and boots, have you?"

"You are asking the wrong person. I am stuck behind the bar all night." She nodded to a waitress walking toward the bar. "You can ask Falda."

A young woman with curly red hair, a pale complexion, and bright smile walked up to the bar with a tray of empty glasses. She spoke to the bartender in Icelandic and faced Hawke. "You are looking for someone?"

"Yes," He repeated the description Riku's father had given him.

"She is with Ásta, Katrín, Bragi, and Sindri." The woman's smile dimmed. "They told me about Nonni. He was a good one."

Hawke found it interesting that Riku was with Nonni's friends. "Where can I find them?"

Falda pointed to a corner. "They are in the corner."

"Thank you." He put a thousand-dollar krona bill on her tray and walked the direction the woman had motioned.

Under one of the lit corner tables sat the three young people he'd met before, plus another young man and two young women. Riku was easy to pick out. She was a pretty Asian girl wearing a red jacket.

Hawke grabbed the closest available chair and placed it at the end of the table.

"We were wondering if you would speak with us," Katrín said, half smiling.

He nodded and stuck out his hand to Riku. "I'm Hawke, your father was one of my class attendees today. He told me you knew Nonni."

The girl barely touched his hand and nodded. "He texted me that you would be coming."

Hawke studied the young woman between Riku and Bragi. "Are you one of Nonni's friends as well?"

She shook her head. "I never met him. This is my first time coming to Iceland." Her accent was a lot like Reggie Carlton's.

"Where are you from? Are you visiting by yourself?"

The young woman stared at him.

"Go ahead and tell him. He is working with the police to figure out who killed Nonni," Ásta said, her words were shaky and her eyes glittered with unshed tears.

"Guinevere Ralston. My friends call me Ginny. I'm here with my family. Father is participating in the SAR conference. I met Riku when we were going to go to dinner tonight."

"Thank you." He shifted his gaze to Riku. "Your father said you met Nonni when you came here two years ago. Are there any other young people at the conference this year who were here then?"

She shook her head. "Not that I have seen."

"What does two years ago have to do with Nonni's death?" Katrín asked.

Hawke shrugged. "Probably nothing. Nonni escorted family members around, and I find it odd that his death happened as this conference was starting." He studied each of the young man's friends. "It seems more likely if someone wanted him dead, they would have found a time when there were less law enforcement officials around."

They all nodded.

"But I don't understand why anyone would want to kill Nonni," Sindri, the young man Hawke hadn't met yet, said.

"That's what I wanted to talk to all of you about. You can't think of anyone who had a problem with Nonni?" He continued to study the young people.

Each one shook their head.

"He was nice to everyone. If you were down, he was the one who picked you up. He had a way of making you look at the bright side of everything," Ásta said.

"That's right. When I was here last time, a friend I made, Wanza, she was in a bad place. That was why her mother brought her with her to the conference. Wanza had wanted to stay home. But once she met Nonni and his friends, she smiled and forgot her problems. She was very happy when she went home. I was sorry she did not come this year." Riku picked at a button on her jacket.

"Did you two stay in touch?" Hawke asked.

"For a few months after the conference, then she stopped texting. I hope she didn't go back to the dark place she had been before."

"Where was she from?" Hawke didn't think a young woman becoming happy here would have anything to do with a death, but he liked to keep his options open.

"Africa somewhere." Riku shook her head. "I

could never say the name."

"It was Macha something," Bragi said.

Katrín bumped his shoulder with hers. "That's right, you two hooked up."

Hawke understood the meaning of hooked up from his earlier conversation with Leonard and the bus driver. They'd had sex. He didn't understand going to bed with someone you barely knew. Even as a young man, he didn't do the deed with a girl unless they had been going steady a while. He wanted to ask how old Wanza had been, but refrained, knowing that he could lose their help if he appeared judgmental.

"On the surface, all of you believe there was no one who hated Nonni enough to kill him?" He scanned all the faces.

"Everyone loved him," Ásta said, her eyes downcast at her drink.

"Don't get mad at me with my next questions, but they have to be asked." He peered each one in the face, all but the new girl, Ginny. "Was he involved in drugs or anything else that could have brought trouble to him?"

They all laughed.

"We liked to come out and drink and dance, but Nonni was the one who told us if we did drugs, he would not be our friend anymore." Katrín gripped Ásta and Sindri's hands. "He had an older brother who overdosed on drugs. He made us vow to never touch the stuff." A tear trickled down her cheek.

The young man Hawke had liked right off was becoming even more and more likeable. Shit! Who had ended this young man's life so soon?

He shifted his conversation to Riku. "Someone told

me that Nonni was talking to a young Asian woman this morning in the restaurant here."

Her eyes filled with tears. "It was me. He was excited about the hike he was taking for your class. I told him he could tell me all about it tonight when we had dinner." She hiccupped and swiped at the tears on her cheeks.

"Think hard. Did he tell you where he was going?"

She shook her head. "I say to him, if you tell me where you are going, I can come too. He said, no. It was a secret between him and Hawke."

The young man had kept his promise and not told anyone. So how had the killer found him? It was looking more and more like a random act. But that conclusion wasn't correct. In his gut, Hawke knew the young man had been sought out and killed. But by who and why? He studied each of the friends who had been in the bar the night before. He and Nonni had kept their voices low as they'd discussed the area, Hawke had wanted the tracking to be done. Had one of them overheard? They all looked sincerely upset over their friend's passing.

"Was anyone sitting nearby when you were talking with him?" he asked Riku.

"I know there were people at some of the tables near us, but I do not know who they were. I was happy to see Nonni and talk with him."

Hawke had a thought. "Did you two schedule to meet for breakfast?"

"No. I happened to see him in the lobby, and we went to the restaurant to visit."

He glanced at the friends. "Did Nonni stay in the hotel during the conference?"

Ásta shook her head. "No. He lives not that far."

"Why was he at the hotel so early?" Hawke said out loud. The group all stared at him, their heads gently moving back forth as if in answer to his question.

"Thank you for your time. If you could all put my name and phone number into your phones and call me if you think of anything, I would appreciate it." He waited for them to all pull out their phones and he rattled off his number.

"Aren't the Reykjavik Police handling this?" Bragi asked.

"Yes. I'm just helping them. Everything you told me will be given to them, and they give me everything they hear." He knew it wasn't his call to add the next thing but it didn't hurt to have whoever killed the young man realize the police were working overtime to find the killer. "We have to figure out who did this before the conference ends. If the killer is a conference attendee, we have to find the truth before everyone goes home."

Chapter Seven

Following up on the fact Nonni was in the hotel early that morning, Hawke decided to see if he'd been there to see someone. It appeared everyone had known the young man. If he had been here, then someone should know why.

He walked out to the registration desk and asked if anyone from the morning shift was available.

"Only the manager is still here," the young woman at the counter said.

"May I speak to the manager?" Hawke hadn't shown any credentials.

"What is this about?" she asked, picking up the phone.

"Jón Einarsson."

The woman's face puckered a moment before she caught herself and spoke into the phone. All he understood was the young man's name.

When she put the receiver down, he asked, "Did

you know Nonni?"

"Yes. He was in my class in school. Always happy. Always making everyone feel better. I can't believe someone would—"

Before she could finish, a woman entered behind the desk. "Sara, go back to your work."

The young woman nodded and turned her back on them.

Hawke held out his hand, "Hawke. Ma'am, I'm helping the Reykjavik police gather information about Jón Einarsson."

The woman led him over to two chairs out of hearing of the main lobby. "You are not Icelandic."

"No, I work for the Oregon State Police, back in the States. I happen to be the person Nonni was working with when he, well, when things went wrong. I feel a bit responsible and am helping the police gather information to find out who could have done this."

"I see. And why did you want to talk with me?" The woman was in her fifties, about average height, brown hair with a sprinkling of gray, and hazel eyes that snapped with authority.

"I learned that Nonni was in the lobby early this morning. A friend of his saw him and they had breakfast together in the restaurant. Do you happen to know why he was here?"

"When he picked up people for his tours or dinners, he would wait for them in the lobby."

"But he didn't have one of those this morning." Hawke studied the woman. Was she being evasive on purpose or was she stalling for some reason?

"He would sometimes come in ahead of time and let us know when he would be picking people up. I believe he was to take a group to dinner tonight at the Perlan. He might have been arranging that."

"Who would he have spoken to about that?"

"Whoever was at the desk."

"Could you look the person up and let me know if they will be working tomorrow morning?" He waited as she stood, walked to the desk, flipped a page, and returned.

"It was Grady. He will be here in the morning at six."

"Thank you. I'll be here." Hawke stood and walked out onto the sidewalk. The brisk walk back to his hotel helped him put what he'd learned into compartments in his brain. The first and foremost was the fact that they had a murder victim who, by all accounts, had no reason to be murdered.

A man in his forties stood behind the desk at the Marina Hotel at 6:15 am when Hawke entered the lobby. He'd awakened at 5:30 after five hours of sleep. He'd gone over all of his notes before going to sleep the night before. At six, he'd left his room and walked to the hotel. He planned to talk to the desk clerk and then have breakfast in the restaurant and visit with the people who had been in his outing yesterday.

"May I help you?" the man at the desk, Grady, the manager had called him, asked.

"I hope so." Hawke held out his hand and introduced himself. "I'm helping the local police discover what happened to Jón Einarsson."

The man shook his head. "I heard about it on the news last night. I couldn't believe it." The man was American.

"You knew him?" Hawke had learned over the years more came from a conversation when you let the other person talk and just listened.

"Yeah. He and his friends come here a lot. And then there's the conference. They move the sites around, but there are usually people who are attending the conference that stay here. Nonni always came around, gathering up the families for outings."

Hawke nodded. "Was that what he was doing here yesterday morning?"

The man stared at him. "How did you…" He gave a half nod. "Because you're investigating his death." He rubbed a hand across the back of his neck. "Man, I don't get it. They say it was murder. Everyone liked Nonni. It doesn't make sense."

"So I've been told. What about yesterday morning? Who did he talk to?"

Grady tapped the pen he held on the counter. "He came to me, said he'd be picking up members of the Tanaka, Ralston, and Riddicci families and a Ms. Pearce around six. Then he met Ms. Tanaka and walked to the restaurant. After that I don't know."

"Did everyone in the family usually go to the dinners and events with Nonni?" Hawke wondered at the comments Riku had made the night before. It sounded as if Nonni had taken the younger members of the family out clubbing.

"Dinners usually. Then the parents and younger members would come back and Nonni would take those old enough clubbing." He smiled. "There is nothing like the Icelandic nightlife."

"So I've heard. Thank you." Hawke headed to the restaurant. He wanted to visit with Riku some more. He wondered if something had happened during a clubbing incident. It appeared Nonni took pride in taking care of people. Had someone perhaps tried something with a conference attendee's family member and when he intervened put a target on his back?

Hawke shook his head. He liked it better when he had footprints and nature to help him discover what happened. Talking to people and trying to piece together the young man's habits wasn't near as easy as reading signs in the wilderness.

He sat at a table and sipped coffee, slowly eating the breakfast he'd gathered from the buffet. Several people who were part of the conference wandered in. They hadn't been in his workshop yesterday. He knew them as conference attendees by the conference tag dangling from lanyards around their necks.

Carlton entered the restaurant. He scanned the room, spotted Hawke, filled a tray with food, and walked his direction.

"Mind if I take a seat?" he asked.

Hawke shoved a chair back with his foot. "Take a load off."

The Englishman chuckled. "You Yanks are cowboys all the time."

"Not a good analogy. I'm Native American. My ancestors didn't care much for cowboys. I'd rather be called straight forward."

"I'm such a plonker. I didn't mean to make you upset."

"I'm not upset. Just setting you straight."

"Did you learn anything more about Nonni's death?" The man poured himself a cup of coffee from the carafe Hawke had asked the waitress to leave on the table.

"Nope. Should have information from the autopsy when I meet with Sigga and Böðvarsson later." He hoped something would show if the murder had been planned and a weapon had been taken with the killer, or it had been unintentional or spur of the moment.

"Nonni's friends know of any enemies?" Carlton sipped his coffee.

"Nope." He studied the other man. "You hear anything from the other attendees?"

"No. Everyone who has been here before is in shock. Can't believe it." Carlton shook his head. "I called home and told my daughter. She was here two years ago and had a good time with Nonni and his friends. She started crying. That was how the young man affected people. Everyone he met loved him."

"Someone didn't."

Carlton's eyes widened. He stared at Hawke. "I guess you're right there."

"Did your daughter happen to mention a girl named Wanza two years ago?" Hawke didn't know why but since the others brought her up, it had been in the back of his mind.

"The name sounds familiar. I'll call her later and ask." Carlton sipped his coffee, studied him over the rim, and asked, "Do you think this was a random killing? He came across someone who didn't want to be found?"

Hawke didn't want to give away what little they knew, but the man seemed to genuinely care. "From the tracks I followed, it wasn't random. The killer hiked back to the car park. Someone who was out by the mud pool and didn't want to be seen wouldn't have hiked to such a public place."

The man nodded. "That makes sense. More sense than anything else about this."

Hawke nodded and spotted Ms. Tumaini and Mayta entering the restaurant. When the Australian glanced his way, he waved and motioned to the two seats at his table. She nodded.

"Gathering the troops, are you?" Carlton asked, catching sight of who Hawke waved at.

"Just want a few more answers." He noticed Ms. Tumaini shake her head, when Mayta must have mentioned sitting with him. But the two walked over and took the last two open seats at the table after putting food on their trays.

"G'day," Mayta said, placing her plate, utensils, and cup of coffee on the table and setting the tray on another table.

"Good morning," Carlton said, cheerfully.

Hawke just nodded and sipped his coffee trying not to study the African woman. She nervously removed her dishes, not once making eye contact.

"Ready to learn more today?" Mayta asked.

"About SAR or Nonni's death?" Carlton asked.

Mayta stared at the other man then at Hawke. "Are you both diggin into that?"

"No. Just me." Hawke kept a peripheral gaze on the other woman. She shoved her food around on the plate. "You haven't said anything this morning," he said, acknowledging Ms. Tumaini.

She glanced up and smiled half-heartedly. "Nothing to say. I want to eat and get to my seminar."

"Did you know the young man, Nonni?" Hawke watched her.

This time she stared back at him. "I told you yesterday. I had not met the person before. This is my first time at this conference."

"Why didn't you want to come sit with us?" Hawke decided to hit her straight on with what he saw.

Her eyes narrowed. "Because I have seen your kind before. You judge us all before you even know us." She slammed her dishes back on her tray, stood, and walked over to another table.

"Good job, Yank. You made her steam." Carlton slapped him on the back.

"Is pissin people off your way of gettin at the truth?" Mayta asked, grinning and biting into a piece of toast.

"It's interesting that she would accuse me of the same thing my ancestors, and myself included, have felt toward people with lighter skin than mine." Hawke wondered at the woman's comment. He didn't know much about Africa. Guess he'd better check out the political atmosphere there.

Leonard Harlow entered the restaurant. He filled a tray and glanced around the room. His gaze landed on them and he strode over, with tray in hand.

Mayta groaned.

Hawke chuckled to himself. His phone buzzed. Böðvarsson. He would have enjoyed watching the young American irritate Mayta, but he had a homicide to investigate. "Gotta go." He stood.

"Will you be at any of the seminars?" Mayta asked.

"Doubt it." He answered the phone and strode to the door.

Chapter Eight

Böðvarsson asked Hawke to come to the conference base of operations at the Harpa. He strode down the street toward the glass structure as rain drizzled, and wind made the day feel colder than it was. Holding his hat on his head, he entered the Harpa and shook. Water splattered onto the floor. He cautiously walked across the tile floor to the staircase.

The detective hadn't mentioned any leads, only to come to the conference headquarters to compare notes. Hawke had made copies of his notes at the copy machine in his hotel.

Shoving the door open to the small room used as conference headquarters, Hawke was surprised to see Nonni's father.

"Mr.—" He caught Sigga shaking her head. "Einar, I'm surprised to see you here."

"I have a conference to run. Nonni wouldn't have

wanted it to stop because of him. He loved helping with this event. And my second in command seems to have become overwhelmed when put in control." The man swiped a hand across his eyes. "I needed something to keep my mind busy."

That Hawke understood. When his wife divorced him, he had dug into work as if it were the only thing that would sustain him. Not dwelling on the fact his job was the reason his wife left. Putting in even more time helped him to get over the anger and grief. Not so much for his wife, but the institution of marriage. She'd picked her drug-selling brother over her husband.

Sigga broke into his thoughts. "Did you learn anything else since we saw you last?"

He relayed his conversation with Riku and Nonni's friends. "None of them can think of any reason anyone would want to kill Nonni." He glanced at Einar who had his back to the conversation. After hearing he'd lost one son to a drug overdose, Hawke's heart went out to the man who'd lost a second in another tragic way.

Einar faced them. "I remember something about Wanza. Nonni had talked about her at home. She wasn't happy with her life. Her mother had made it as far up the ranks of the Nairobi police as she could get being a woman. Wanza wanted to get out of Africa. Go to college here or in America. I know Nonni was giving her as much information as he could find."

"Did he stay in contact with her after she left?" Hawke wasn't sure what an acquaintance from Africa would have but he was willing to look at anything.

"Ari, send a policeman over to my house. I'll have my wife get Nonni's computer ready." Einar pulled out his cellphone.

They hadn't found the young man's phone. "Do you know where Nonni's phone is?"

Einar shook his head. "He always had it with him."

"It's probably being dissolved by that *leirhver*, mud pool," Sigga said.

Hawke had the same thought. It could have been in the young man's hand or loose in his coat pocket and been sucked down into the mud and water. He handed the photocopies of his notes over to Sigga and Böðvarsson.

"This is what we've learned so far," the inspector said, handing Hawke a thin file folder.

He opened the file and sat at a table to read the contents.

The forensic pathologist believed Nonni was hit on the head with a piece of lava and landed face first in the steaming pool. A laceration was found on the back of his head that could have propelled his body forward. Given his position in the water, he would have been facing the pool and most likely not even seen his assailant, unless he'd turned his back on them, not believing they were a threat.

"Did CID pick up any rocks with blood or hair on them?" he asked. Lava would be hard to get prints off and given the weather yesterday, it was a sure bet the assailant was wearing gloves.

"They found one. Halla is going to see if it fits today." Böðvarsson flicked a glance toward Einar.

Hawke had gathered the two were friends and talking about his son's death like this had to be hard on both men. He flipped by the coroner's report and studied the information on the license plates he'd written down in the parking lot. The three rental cars were rented to people visiting. One was highlighted. He put his finger on the name. "Does this mean they are part of the conference?"

Sigga leaned over his shoulder. "Yes. Kevin Largess from Louisiana. When I talked to him, he said he was in the other pre-conference seminar and didn't use his car, but he must have dropped his keys somewhere because they were slid under the door of his room when he entered after dinner last night."

"Was he here two years ago?" Hawke wrote the name down in his notebook.

"Yes," Einar said. "He's been here the last three conferences. He is a climbing instructor."

"He knew your son?" Hawke asked.

"Yes. We had Kevin over for dinner last year. He and Nonni had a good time discussing American Pop Culture." A wistful smile tipped the corners of the man's mouth. "Nonni was saving money to make a trip to America. He wanted to see the cities we hear about and see on television. And he was fascinated by your large trees and woodlands."

Sadness squeezed Hawke's chest. He could have taken Nonni horse packing in the Wallowas. He shoved that thought aside. "Where can I find Largess?"

"I already talked to him," Sigga said, placing her hands on her hips.

"I don't think you didn't do your job. I prefer to see people's reactions when I talk to them." Hawke stood.

"You'll have to find a car. He's onsite at Mount Skessuhorn," Einar said.

"I'll take you. My car is at the car park near Hotel Marina," Sigga said.

Hawke nodded. "Will you know if any more evidence has been collected from the rock or the area when I get back?" he asked Böðvarsson.

"If we're lucky, we should have more. But don't get your hopes up. The rain and terrain made it hard to collect much."

Shoving his arms into his coat, Hawke contemplated all he knew. "Any chance you could get a list of the names of the family members who would have been old enough to go clubbing with Nonni since he became of that age?" He directed this to Einar.

"I can try."

He glanced at Böðvarsson. "And see if you can get the paperwork to have a CID team go over Largess's rental."

Sigga headed for the door. "I need to get a warmer coat. Do you have anything warmer?"

"No. This is it."

She shrugged. "It can be cold if we have to go to the top to speak to Kevin."

"I'll buy a stocking cap in one of the shops here while you go get your car," he said as they descended the stairs to the main floor.

"Better to buy a cap and come with me." She led him to one of the shops. "This one will not be as expensive as the other one."

At a small display of stocking caps, he picked one that looked hand knitted. After paying, he shoved it in his pocket. He'd feel silly carrying his Stetson and wearing the stocking cap. He could leave his hat in Sigga's car and wear the stocking cap when they arrived at the mountain.

Two and a half hours later, Sigga pulled into a parking lot at the base of a mostly bare mountain. Hawke set his cowboy hat in the back seat and molded the stocking cap to his head. He was glad to get out and walk. His legs were cramped from riding in the small car. He wanted space between him and the inquisitive woman. The last two hours all she did was ask him questions about where he lived, how he liked his job, and about his family. He only answered half her questions, feeling she was too nosy.

"That's the bus that brought the rock-climbing class here." Sigga pointed at a bus a lot like the one that had taken them to track Nonni.

"Do you know where they are climbing at?" He didn't see anyone scaling the rocky mountainside.

"They should have finished lunch and are starting to climb the northwest ridge. We can take the chance they will come back that way or hike to the top on a trail and hope to catch Kevin before they start back down the cliff." Sigga pulled water bottles out of her trunk, handing him two and putting two in her small day pack.

Hawke slipped the water into his pack. "Thanks. I say we hike to the base of the cliff and wait for them to come back down."

She nodded and headed off on a well-worn path. Hawke stayed several yards behind her, he preferred to enjoy the outdoors by himself. The past sixteen years, he'd spent days alone in the Eagle Cap Wilderness, checking hunting licenses and looking for poachers. Those days were the reason he didn't take many vacations. Who needed a vacation when you spent so much quality time on the mountains?

Fox Goes Hunting

He studied the mountains ahead of him. They were sparse, bearing small trees that looked nothing like the majestic pine, fir, and tamarack in the Wallowa Mountains. The rock appeared more solid basalt and lava than the lime, shale, and granite he was used to seeing in slides and boulders on the mountains back home.

"You are quiet back there. Are you regretting wasting time coming here?" Sigga asked, stopping and pulling a water bottle out of her pack.

"I won't know if this is a waste until I talk to Largess." He pulled out a water bottle and sipped, hoping the woman would continue on.

"Why do you call everyone by their last name? Is it because you go by your last name?" She capped the bottle and stared at him.

"I only call men by their last names. I learned it in the Army and it stuck." He shoved his bottle back in his pack and strode around her, following the trail. In front, he could keep a fast pace and keep her from asking questions.

Unfortunately, by walking fast they had time to kill waiting for the rock climbers to return. A climber dropped over the edge of the rim as Hawke set down his pack and took a seat on a smooth rock. One that had been used by many to sit and watch or wait.

"Do you think Kevin really had something to do with Nonni's death?" Sigga remained standing, staring up at the cliff.

"I won't know until I talk to him. It is convenient to say you didn't even know your car was missing. His car was used to transport the killer. Of that I'm certain. Nothing else explains why it was there and the keys were returned under his door."

The climbers, one by one, made their way down to one ledge after another until the group had all descended to the area where Hawke and Sigga sat.

"Sigga, what are you doin' here?" a tall, muscular black man asked, walking over to Sigga and giving her a one-armed hug.

"Looking for you." Sigga put an arm around his waist and faced Hawke. "Hawke is helping us with Nonni's homicide. He has some questions for you."

The man frowned and stuck out a hand.

Hawke shook, noting the man's firm grip.

"You didn't have to come clear out here. We would have been back by dinner time." Largess motioned to a man helping the others. "Tony, get everyone's gear rounded up and head back to the bus." The other man waved an arm.

"Let's walk back." Largess kept his arm around Sigga.

They walked with Sigga on one side of the man and Hawke on the other. He would have preferred to stay still and watch the man better, but he also understood the need to get the attendees back to the bus before dark.

"I understand your rental car was missing yesterday," Hawke started.

"I don't know that it was missing. The keys were missing, but I only know that because they showed up shoved under my door." Largess, ran his free hand over his curly cropped hair. "I didn't know my car was missing until Sigga asked me about it last night." His eyes softened and his lips curved into a smile as he glanced at the woman. Her cheeks deepened in color.

"When did you last use the car?" Hawke asked.

"I drove it from the rental lot to the hotel on Tuesday. I parked it and didn't plan to use the car again until Saturday when I went to dinner at Einar's house."

"Where were the keys to the car? Did you have them in a pocket?"

"No. I tossed them on the glass counter in my hotel room. Someone would have had to come into my room and get them. I know I didn't drop them anywhere."

That was what Hawke wanted to know. How the keys had been taken. "Did anyone visit you in your room? Or did you tell anyone your plans?"

Largess grinned wide, showing off his even white teeth. "I invited several ladies to my room Tuesday night. They were all here early for the pre-conference events."

"Did you get all of their names?" Hawke asked.

The man shook his head. "It was an informal event." He chuckled. "I was walking down the hall and these lovely ladies were standing out in the hall talking. I invited them into my room and we ended up visiting for a couple hours before everyone wandered out."

Hawke shook his head. "Did you get any of their names?"

"The blonde Aussie. A German girl. I really remember their countries more than their names. That's what we talked about. The differences and similarities among our countries." The man shrugged.

The Aussie had to be Mayta. Hawke hoped she had a better memory than this guy.

Chapter Nine

As soon as they arrived back at the Harpa, Hawke headed to the conference headquarters to get a phone number for Mayta. He was directed to Einar to vouch he could get the number before it was given to him.

"Why do you need her phone number?" Einar asked.

Hawke studied the man. Did he dare let him in on the investigation? He wasn't sure how much Böðvarsson had told the father of the murder victim. "I need to ask her a few more questions that have come up."

"Do you think she killed Nonni? I don't see how. They had never met." Einar didn't say it as if to discount the idea but more as if he was feeling Hawke out.

"I don't know who did it. I only know she was at a gathering where I would like to know the names of all the people." Hawke wasn't going to divulge any more than that.

"I see." Einar stared at him and finally waved a hand to the woman who had been waiting for him to agree to give out the phone number. "Give him the number."

She typed on a computer and recited the number.

Hawke wrote it down in his notebook next to Mayta's name. "Thank you." He left the room and dialed the number. He hadn't expected her to answer and left a message. "This is Hawke. Give me a call or text when you are available to talk."

He hung up and found a quiet corner with a chair and pulled out the file Böðvarsson had handed him that morning. Now it was time to go over it carefully. He would have read it all on the drive to see Largess but Sigga had kept asking questions, not allowing him to fall into the information.

Opening the folder, he started at the top of the first page and read, writing notes in the side bar of his notebook. All the attendees that were here Tuesday and attended pre-conference events on Wednesday had been interviewed. The ones that had known Nonni from past conferences had only good things to say. Those that had yet to meet him, could be marked off as not having anything to do with his murder.

His phone buzzed as people flowed out into the hallway from the meeting rooms. "Hawke."

"You want to meet?" Mayta asked.

"Yeah. But some place quiet where we can talk. How about the lobby in my hotel? It's just across the street." He didn't want to go to a bar or hang out here where people would start socializing since it was the end of the day.

"Fine by me."

"I'll be down outside the doors to the Harpa," he said, ending the conversation as Ms. Pearce walked up to him.

"People were bummed you didn't continue your class today." She stared at him with disapproval on her face.

"It didn't seem right to go over details of the trip that didn't end with good results." He stood, shouldered his pack, and walked away. Interesting. Were there really people who had wanted him to go over what little they'd learned or had Ms. Pearce just started a conversation for another reason? Stopping at the top of the staircase, he glanced over to where he'd left the woman. She was looking at her phone.

He continued down the stairs and out to the sidewalk in front of the opera house/conference center. Less than five minutes later, Mayta emerged from the doors. She spotted him and walked up to his side.

"You look like you could use a stubbie. Sure you don't want to hit a bar?"

"I'm sure. You can go after I talk to you if you want." He led her across the multiple lane main road and the side road to get to his hotel. Inside the doors, he turned left and took the two steps down to the small lobby area. The chairs and couches were low with wide seats and short backs. The cushions were thick but the chairs didn't fit most people.

Mayta, however, kicked off her boots and curled her feet up under her as she took a seat. Hawke sat on a chair to the side of the couch the woman lounged on.

"Do you remember attending a gathering in your

hotel on Tuesday night in Kevin Largess's room?"

"Kevin? Oh, the climbin trainer. Yeah, we were havin a bit of a yak in the hall when he arrived and invited us in."

"Can you name all the people who went in his room?" Hawke had his notebook open on his lap.

She glanced at the book. "Why are you askin?"

"It's part of the investigation." He could tell she wanted more, but he wasn't divulging.

"You don't think Kevin did it? He's a larrikin but he'd never harm anyone."

"Larrikin?" It was Hawke's turn to stare at her like she was crazy.

"Larrikin, a bloke who likes to have a good time, play a prank."

"Yeah, I got that feeling from him, too. Who besides you two were in the room?" He persisted.

"Hilda, I didn't get her last name. I think she's from Germany. Nancy from the States. We all had rooms in that hall. We met coming back from dinner."

"What level and room number are you?" He could easily get a list of the rooms and people in them.

"Second floor. Two-thirty."

"Do you have more names of those present?"

She scowled. "Carmilla from Italy, Rowena from England, I think. She was with Kanika." She closed her eyes. "There was someone else, but I can't remember her name." Her eyelids raised and she peered into his face. "Does that help?"

"Yes. I'll see if the others have any recollection of the person you don't remember." He closed his notebook. He'd need to go back across to the conference headquarters and get the phone numbers of the other women. "I can walk you back to the Harpa."

"Are you goin' to the dinner tonight?" She stood.

"What dinner?"

"The one for those of us who've been here the last two days for pre-conference." She stared at him as if he were dimwitted.

There was a good chance he'd bump into the ladies. "Sure. And you can point out the ladies you just mentioned."

She grinned. "Does that make you my date?"

"No." He shouldered his pack and motioned for her to head out of the hotel.

Hawke followed Mayta to the elevator. She hit the third floor button. There was one other couple in the elevator. They appeared to be husband and wife. They were talking in a language Hawke couldn't decipher.

They exited the elevator and walked along a short hall and into a room set up with tables and a long buffet filled with food. "Stay with me so you can point out the women," Hawke said in a low voice.

"If you aren't my date, I can do as I please."

He heard the mischief in the woman's voice. "You are welcome to cling to any man you want after you point the women out."

She scrunched her face and began plucking food from the buffet table.

An elbow in his side almost caused him to drop the plate he'd been filling. "What?"

"That's Nancy, over there at the table in the corner. And just sitting at that table is Carmilla."

Hawke studied the two. "Let's get a table, and I'll go have a chat with them."

"If your runnin off after other women, I'm not goin to sit at a table waitin for you to prowl on back." She strode over to a table that had Carlton and the Tanaka family.

He noted there was one more open chair. Hawke walked over and placed his plate in that spot. "Be right back," he said to Carlton's raised eyebrows.

At the table with the two women, who also sat with four other women, Hawke directed his attention to the two he was interested in. "Nancy and Carmilla, could I have a word with you?"

They both showed shock that he knew them. They glanced at one another and then around the table.

"I just have a quick question about Tuesday night."

Nancy stood and motioned for Carmilla to follow her. He took the two off to the side of the room where there was less traffic.

"Why do you need to talk to us about Tuesday night?" Nancy asked.

"I'm helping the Reykjavik Police with the homicide of Jón Einarsson. I understand you were in Kevin Largess's room on Tuesday night."

"He did not kill anyone!" Carmilla said, louder than he liked.

"I know he didn't. I need information about the people who were in his room that night."

Nancy peered at him. "Do you think the killer was in the room? We were all women."

"Women do commit eleven percent of murders."

Carmilla now glared at him. "We did not kill anyone."

"I'm not saying you or anyone in the room did. I just want the names, please." He pulled his phone out and opened a text app.

Nancy glanced at his phone and started, "Hilda—I don't know anyone's last name except Carmilla. We're rooming together."

Hawke nodded, his way of saying that's okay and go on.

"Hilda, Carmilla, me, two black women. Rowena, she sounded British, and Kanika, she wasn't British or American. Not sure where she was from. I think they are rooming together. Mayta, the Australian woman. And an Icelander." She turned to Carmilla, "Do you remember her name?"

"It was like cigarette," the Italian said, making the motion of puffing on a cigarette and blowing out the smoke.

Hawke had a suspicion he knew who that Icelander was. "Could it have been Sigga?"

Nancy pointed her finger at him. "That's who it was."

"And she didn't leave when the rest of us did." Carmilla's narrowed eyes and pout expressed she had wished to stay after with the rock-climbing instructor.

"Thank you. You were both helpful." He turned off his phone, shoved it into his shirt pocket, and headed back to the table where his food was getting cold.

"Did they remember who the other woman was?" Mayta asked.

"Yeah." He was beginning to wonder if Chief Inspector Sigga Eiríksdóttir had been helping to hide the real murderer. He knew she didn't kill Nonni. She'd been on the bus and with the group the whole time. But had she stolen a rental car key for someone else?

He dug into his meal, barely listening to the

conversation going on around him. Sigga had said she was staying in the hotel during the conference. Was it to meet up with Kevin? They had given off strong sexual interest for one another when they were all walking back to the bus.

Hawke raised his head and scanned the room. Neither were eating dinner. "Was everyone supposed to come to this dinner?" he asked Carlton.

"No, it isn't mandatory. It is paid for with your conference fee. And they put on a good spread." The man held up a forkful of firm white fish, dripping in a sauce.

Hawke rose.

"Where're you goin'?" Mayta asked.

"I have some phone calls to make."

"Don't you ever relax?" Carlton asked.

Hawke stared at the man, then the woman, and finally the Tanaka family who had been quiet. "I can't relax until I've figured out the motive and who killed Nonni."

"Mr. Hawke, you will miss a nice dessert by leaving," Riku said, quietly.

He glanced at her but couldn't tell if she wanted him to stay to talk to him or was just mentioning the dessert in order to keep him here.

"Thank you, but I need to talk to someone." He excused himself and headed to the elevator. Standing in the small closed-in area of the elevator, he studied his reflection in the stainless-steel wall. His hair was standing up, most likely from the stocking cap he'd worn. Which reminded him, he'd left his Stetson in Sigga's car. Now he had a good reason to look her up at the Marina Hotel.

Chapter Ten

Hawke walked the short distance to the other hotel. The clerk from the night before stood behind the desk.

"Could I have Sigga Eiríksdóttir's room number and Kevin Largess's room number please? I know they are both on the second floor."

The woman looked them up on the computer and rattled off the numbers to him.

"Thank you." He stepped into the elevator and hit the number 2. The trip was barely long enough to sort out which room to visit first. He came to Sigga's first. Knocking on the door, he listened while surveying the hallway. There was a surveillance camera in the middle and at the end of the corridor. He pulled out his phone and texted a message to Böðvarsson to request the surveillance tape for Wednesday afternoon and evening. If they got a look at who placed the key under the door, that would help them find the murderer.

He knocked one more time and moved on down the

hall to Largess's room. Music softly played. Jackpot.

Hawke knocked on the door, louder than he had the previous door. Muffled voices on the other side of the door had him grinning. He knocked again.

"Just a minute!" Largess called out.

Hawke stepped to the side, making it hard for the man to recognize him if he looked out the peephole.

The door opened slightly. Largess's head and shoulder the size of a bowling ball were visible. "What do you want?"

"I need to talk to Sigga." Hawke crossed his arms and waited.

"Why would you think she's here?" The rock climber didn't open the door any further.

"The way you two were cuddling as we walked back to the bus. She's not in her room. And you neglected to name her as one of the women in your room on Tuesday night." Hawke put a hand on the door and gave it a shove. "Care to explain that?" He walked into the room.

Largess had a sheet around his bottom half. Sigga sat in a chair, wearing a robe and her hair all messed up.

"There's nothing to explain. I know she didn't steal my key so why say anything?" Largess sat on the bed closest to where the woman sat.

Hawke stared at Sigga. "When you knew why I wanted to question Kevin, why didn't you tell me you had been here? You could have told me the names of the others."

She shook her disheveled head. "I don't remember who was here. I came in after they were all in the room." She narrowed her eyes at Largess. "I saw Kevin's door open and came down to see what was happening. Turned out he had women in his room. They were all trying to get him to give them an invitation to stay." She smiled and ran a finger down his arm. "I commented he was mine for the night and they all hastily left."

Hawke glanced at the glass counter with fishing lures and knots under the glass. "This is where you left the keys?" A set of keys with the car rental fob sat on the glass top.

"Yes. Just like that."

"And you didn't notice they were missing until they showed up under the door?" Hawke wondered that the man didn't realize they were gone. They were easy to see on the top of the glass.

"I was busy when the others left and hurried to my seminar the next morning." Largess crossed his arms.

"What time did you notice them under the door?" It would help to nail down the time the keys were returned.

"They were on the floor when I opened the door after dinner last night."

"And that time was…?"

"I came back to the room about nine. We were questioned by police, then I went to dinner, had a couple beers, and came back here." He glanced at Sigga. "I tried calling her room, but she didn't answer."

"I know where she was." Hawke held in the smugness he felt as the other man gave Sigga a proprietary glower.

"We were going over all the interviews and what to do next on the case." She quickly added, "Ari was there, too. In the conference base of operations room."

He wondered at the two being so close and fiercely

guarding one another. Glancing between the two of them he asked, "And neither one of you had any problem with Nonni or heard of him having any problems with anyone associated with this conference?"

"I told you earlier. He was a good kid. I have one dinner with his family when I'm here. I wouldn't hurt him and had no reason to." Largess stood, his face growing redder with each word and his voice huskier.

"I thought of Nonni like a younger brother or cousin. He gave me no reason to wish him dead." Sigga also took affront to his asking.

Hawke eased toward the door. "Any chance I can get my hat from you tomorrow?"

Sigga stared at him open-mouthed as if she were ready to cuss him out.

"I'll bring your hat to conference headquarters," Largess said.

Hawke nodded and left the room. He knew the time frame to study the surveillance tape when they received it tomorrow. Other than that, he couldn't think of anything else that he could do tonight.

Walking back to his hotel, his phone buzzed. A text from Riku. *Join us at the Bergmál.*

He was tired and didn't want to go to a bar, but Nonni's friends might inadvertently say something that could shine a light on the young man's death.

Hawke shoved the stocking cap into his coat pocket and ran his hands through his hair before entering the bar on the ground floor of the Harpa. He found the group. The same four Icelandic friends and Riku. The extra young woman from the night before wasn't with them.

He took the empty chair on the end of the booth where the group sat. Sindri and Katrín and Bragi and Riku seemed to have paired off. Leaving Ásta as the fifth wheel in this case.

"You asked me to join you," he said, sitting down and motioning for a waitress. When she appeared, he ordered a beer and returned his attention to the group of young people.

Ásta leaned toward him. "Have you figured out who killed Nonni?" Her wide blue eyes held hope and sorrow.

"We're still working on it." He paid the waitress who had returned with his beer. Taking a sip, he studied each one. They all seemed deflated by his announcement.

Setting the bottle down, he said, "You can't think of anyone who would want to harm him? Even if it was just something small. The right person can make something small into something much larger in their minds."

"He would make fun of people, but not hurtful, more to make them see the humor in themselves." Ásta peered around the table at the others. "There was one boy, I think he was here four years ago. Remember, he was from America. He came with his father."

"Billy Boy, yes!" Sindri joined in. "He thought he was special because his father was high in the police force in a big city."

Katrín laughed. "He was so full of himself you could have filled the Friðheimar hot houses with his hot air."

"What did Nonni do or say that upset Billy?" Hawke took another sip of his beer, refraining from taking notes.

"He told him to use his hot air for something useful, like keeping the people parachuting in the air." Sindri laughed.

Hawke didn't understand. "What do you mean about people parachuting?"

"One of the classes that year was parachuting into hard to land places. Billy's father had been in the military and was teaching the parachuting class even though he hadn't used it for search and rescue where he lived." Ásta studied her hands. "They almost had an accident with the class."

Hawke still didn't understand. "Someone was hurt?"

"No, they discovered the fault before anyone jumped but it was Billy's father's instructions that could have caused several to be injured." Ásta peered at him. "Nonni was the one who discovered the mistake."

"Billy came in here that night and wanted to tear Nonni's head off for making his father look bad," Bragi said.

"Do any of you remember Billy's last name?" He pulled out his phone and added Billy, four years ago, father taught parachuting, US.

They all shook their heads. It was a bit of a lead.

"Has anyone seen him here this year? Either Billy or his father?"

They again shook their heads.

"What about here? Local people?"

"No. We understand humor here and jest with each other all the time." Bragi put an arm around Riku. "Riku and Wanza fit right in last conference."

Hawke studied the two. They seemed friendly, but

he didn't see any sparks coming off either one of them. Not like he'd witnessed with the older couple Sigga and Largess. "Were you two an item then?"

They both shook their heads.

"I fell for Wanza. Something about making her sadness go away." Sadness drooped Bragi's eyes.

"Did you two stay in touch?" Hawke glanced at the others. They understood their friend's sadness.

"I tried. Three months after she went home, she stopped texting. I didn't have her address or remember the name of the town where she lived." Bragi removed his arm from Riku and downed the rest of the drink in his glass.

"She stopped replying to my texts as well," Riku said. Her gaze flit from person to person around the table ending on Hawke. "We all have wondered what happened to her."

Hawke added Wanza to his list of people to remind Einar about in the morning. "Thank you for inviting me and giving me more information about Nonni." He stood.

"You will let us know if you learn anything?" Riku asked.

Ásta's gaze flicked over Riku before she stared at him.

"Yes." He walked out of the bar and across the street to his hotel.

In his room, Hawke wrote down the information he'd put in his phone and what the young people had told him at the bar.

He had three days left to find Nonni's killer before the conference attendees spread around the world.

Chapter Eleven

Dani called at 5 am to ask Hawke about the weather and how the conference was going. They'd visited for half an hour when Dani decided the call was over because she needed to go to bed. He chuckled. She'd woken him up and she wanted to go to sleep.

He ended the call, dressed, checked his notes, and headed to the Harpa, hoping they had coffee and muffins set out in the conference base of operations. The room was empty when Hawke arrived. The scent of coffee filled the air, and he found a pump pot of coffee and a basket of baked goods. Sitting down at a table with the coffee and muffin, he started making notes in the sidebar of his notebook.

"Good morning," the woman who had been in this room the day before when he'd talked to Einar said, as she entered the room.

"Morning." He watched her start up the two computers in the room and walk over to get a cup of coffee. "What do you do for the conference?"

She smiled. "I keep the website up and running, gather the registrations, and set up the classes."

"All of that is before the conference. What do you do now, while it's running?" Hawke stood, stretched, and walked over to refill his cup.

"I make sure the tech people get the right equipment in the right rooms, record the courses that are being recorded, and help people remember what they signed up for." She sat down at the larger of the two computers.

"How long have you worked for the conference?"

"Eight years." She tapped keys and several screens came to life.

"Could you get me information on some people from past conferences?"

She stared at him. "With Einar's permission."

"When will he arrive?" Hawke returned to his seat and sipped his coffee.

The woman glanced at her watch. "In about an hour."

An hour to sit here and twiddle his thumbs.

"You could call and ask him for permission." The woman hadn't looked up from the computer. Had he made a sound that gave away his frustration?

"His number?" Hawke held his phone in his hand.

She dictated the numbers, Hawke dialed, and Einar answered.

"Halló?"

"Einar, this is Hawke. I would like you to give permission to the woman in the conference headquarters to give me names and phone numbers of some past attendees."

The man sputtered. "Past attendees. What would that have to do with Nonni's death?"

"Possibly nothing. I visited with his friends last night and learned of an altercation four years ago with someone named Billy—"

"That was nothing. It all blew over." Einar protested too much.

"I would still like to talk to this Billy. And a young woman who was here last year. Wanza?"

"I don't see that either of those could have anything to do with who murdered my son now." Einar's stubbornness caused Hawke to wonder what either of these might have to do with the death.

"Will you give your computer tech permission to give me this information?" Hawke waited what seemed like more than the couple of minutes as the man made his decision.

"Hand the phone to Dóra."

Hawke did as he was told and waited for the two to talk in Icelandic. That they were concealing what they said from him, made him even more curious about the two names he wanted.

Dóra handed the phone back to him. "I have been given permission to help you."

He listened, realized the man had ended the conversation, and faced the woman sitting at the computer. "Do you know who I want information about?"

She nodded. "Wanza was here with her mother two years ago. Their last name is Odenyo." She typed some more. "This is the number of the mother."

Hawke wrote down the mother's name and phone number. "Thank you. And Billy?"

The woman pursed her lips. "You do not want to stir this up."

"What do you mean?" He pulled a chair over near Dóra and sipped his coffee.

"Billy's father brought a lawsuit against the conference, blaming us for his negligence. That we didn't have the proper equipment ready for his class. We had exactly what he'd asked for. It just happened to not be new because he'd asked for older equipment. Like he'd used when he was in the military."

Hawke nodded. "So, the whole mishap was this man's fault. How could he bring a lawsuit?"

She shook her head. "He is using defamation of character, because Nonni told everyone about how he'd kept this man from killing someone."

"And this is the person who you don't want to give me the name and phone number?" Hawke watched as she mulled over his request. This conference was her job. Did she dare sacrifice it toward finding the person who killed her boss's son?

"Einar wished to not raise the ire of the ogre. Do you think he could have killed Nonni?"

"We won't know until I can find out if he still held a grudge. Four years is plenty of time for him to feel it was water under the bridge." Hawke tried to express empathy toward Einar and Nonni's death, but he always followed every trail, no matter how unpleasant it might be. If he couldn't get the name and phone number from Dóra, he was pretty sure Sigga could help him if she didn't already know about it. If the American police official had sued, there should be a record at a courthouse.

"You won't say anything to get him angry?" Dóra

asked.

"I'll be on my best behavior." Since she didn't know how he rubbed people wrong a lot of the time, she didn't know that was the best he could do.

She handed him a slip of paper with a name and number. "It is the middle of the night there."

"I won't call until after lunch. Thank you." He studied the name. There wasn't a title, just the name and number. That in itself was interesting.

A couple more people arrived, walking straight to the coffee and muffins.

Hawke shoved the name and number in his shirt pocket and walked out into the open loft area. Conference attendees were arriving for their morning classes. Yesterday would have been the end of his class, had he continued it. The next two days he'd planned to sit in on other classes. Now he would be tracking down information.

He pulled out his phone to see what the time was in Kenya. They were three hours ahead. He punched in the number he'd received from Dóra.

The phone rang several times and a message in a language he didn't know come on. The machine beeped and he left a message.

"This is Gabriel Hawke. I'd like to talk to your daughter, Wanza. This is my number, please call me back." He recited his number and ended the call. All he could do was wait.

He called Böðvarsson.

"Ari," the man answered.

"It's Hawke. Are you coming to the conference today?"

"I can. What did you find out?"

"I'll tell you when I see you."

"I'll be there in an hour. Where do you want to meet?"

Hawke scanned the people and conference base of operation's door. "The lobby in the Center Hotel across the street."

"I'll be there."

Hawke wandered down the staircase, out of the building, and across the streets. It was now time for the guests of the hotel to awaken and eat their complimentary breakfast in the upstairs restaurant. He glanced at the uncomfortable chairs in the lobby and sent a text to Böðvarsson to meet him up in the restaurant.

He stepped into the elevator after an older couple stepped out. They smiled. He tipped his head and punched the button for the third floor.

Hawke was on his second cup of coffee and third pastry when Böðvarsson stepped off the elevator. The inspector filled a cup with coffee and helped himself to a pastry before sitting across from Hawke.

"Is there a reason you want to meet here rather than at the Harpa?" Böðvarsson asked, raising the coffee cup to his mouth. "Not that I mind. This is a wonderful view."

Hawke had to agree. He'd been watching the harbor while waiting. "I asked you to come over here because I have a feeling Einar wouldn't like to see me." He shrugged and took a bite of the pastry.

Böðvarsson studied him. "What have you discovered?"

"Not as much as I would like. Four years ago,

Nonni discredited a police official from the US during the man's seminar. Then he taunted, I guess would be the word, the man's son. I learned this morning that the man in question has tried to sue the conference. I need to talk to him or see if he or the son are here, in Reykjavik or Iceland."

Böðvarsson held out his hand. "Give me the names. I can run them and see if they have arrived. That will lessen any contact with them."

Hawke studied the man. "You won't just shove this to the side because it makes Einar uncomfortable?"

"We have few murders on Iceland. I want to get this solved as much as you do. Even more so. It would be a poor mark on my career if I did not catch who did this."

Hearing the truth in the man's words, Hawke pulled the paper out of his pocket. He unfolded it and stared at the name of Wanza's mother. "Is there a chance you can discover more about this woman and her daughter?"

The inspector took the paper. "Where are they located?"

"Kenya. I left a message on her phone."

"Did you already call the man in America?"

"No. I didn't want to piss him off by calling in the middle of the night."

"Good idea. I'll have both of these people looked into. Why do you think this woman would know anything about Nonni's death?"

"I don't. But her daughter's name keeps getting mentioned from the conference two years ago." He let out a deep sigh. "And I can't find anything else other than the keys. Did you get the surveillance tapes from the hotel?"

"I was going to call you once I arrived at the police station to tell you they were available." Böðvarsson finished off his pastry and wiped his mouth and hands. "I can take you if you like."

Hawke finished off his coffee. "I'm ready." He picked up his pack and followed the inspector to the elevator.

Chapter Twelve

By noon, Hawke's eyes were blurry and felt as if he'd been riding in a dust storm. He'd gone over and over the surveillance tape for the time frame the keys would have been slipped under the door and didn't see anything. People came and went up and down the hall. He stopped looking when Largess entered his room. The man said he'd picked up the keys when he'd entered. How had they been left when no one stopped at his door or did anything unusual?

He shoved away from the monitor and wandered down the hall to the restroom. All the coffee he'd consumed had been expanding his bladder the last hour and he'd ignored it.

The only possibility had to be the key was left earlier. Or later!

Largess hadn't stopped when entering the room. Which meant he hadn't picked anything up off the floor. Could the man have walked in, went into the bathroom, and when he came out spotted the key and figured he'd stepped over it on his way in?

Hawke finished and hurried back to the desk and monitor where Böðvarsson had set him up. He let the tape roll after Largess entered the room.

A woman dressed in the hotel uniform bent at the door, straightened, and then walked down the hall, passing the Italian woman, Carmilla, who walked up to Largess's door and knocked.

Now he had something to work with. He spun in his chair and caught the attention of the female officer in the room. "Can I get a photo of the maid and the woman knocking on the door?"

The officer placed the two photos in his hand ten minutes later.

"Where's Böðvarsson's office?" he asked.

The woman showed him down the hall to the door with the man's name on it.

"Thank you." He knocked and walked in.

Sigga sat in the chair in front of the inspector's desk. What would she do when she saw the Italian woman knocking on her lover's door?

"*Sæll*, Hawke, I heard you were looking at surveillance tapes," Sigga said.

"It appears either one of the hotel staff put the key under the door, or a female guest of Largess's dropped it on her way in." Hawke watched Sigga.

Her facial features turned to stone and her eyes glinted with anger.

He wasn't going to let her see the tapes or tell her who. They might have another murder on their hands. "I'm going to go talk to the staff member at the hotel."

His gaze drifted to Böðvarsson and back to Sigga. "Want to give me a lift and give me my hat back?"

She shot out of the chair as if it had ejected her. "Yes. I will give you a ride."

And, no doubt, try to find out who the woman was spending time with her boy toy. Hawke motioned for her to exit the office. When she'd walked out, he closed the door behind her and faced the inspector. "Did you get anywhere with the names I gave you?"

"Not yet. I'll let you know when I do."

Hawke nodded as Sigga opened the door. "Come on!"

He grinned at Böðvarsson and followed the woman out of the building and to her car. Once they were settled in the car, she started interrogating him.

"Tell me the woman who went to Kevin's room." She had her gaze on him and not the road.

"Watch the traffic. Staring at me isn't going to get you the answer. Especially, if we end up in a hospital." He'd already folded up the photo of Carmilla and put it in his pocket. The only one she could try to look at was of the staff member.

"Why won't you tell me who it was?" She pulled her car into the valet parking at the hotel.

"Because you are emotionally involved. I don't want you to scare the person off until I can talk to her." He grabbed his hat from the back seat and plopped it on his head when he stood next to the car. "Forget that while we talk to the staff."

"I am a professional." She huffed, flashing her badge at the valet who walked toward them. She strode by the flustered young man and through the front door.

"Is this you being professional?" Hawke grinned.

This woman was as much fun to pick on as his friend Justine, a waitress at his favorite place for breakfast.

She stopped halfway to the registration counter, pivoted, and glared at him.

Hawke burst out laughing. Thirty seconds ticked by and she started laughing.

"Sorry. That man makes me crazy every year." She drew in a deep breath, let it out, and spun back around.

They walked up to the counter together. Grady, the man he'd visited with the morning before, smiled at him.

Hawke placed the photo of the staff member on the desk. "Is this person working this morning?"

"Is she in trouble?" Grady asked.

"No. We just need to ask her some questions," Hawke motioned to Sigga, who showed her Icelandic police badge.

Grady shook his head. "Tinna comes in to work when I go home. She won't be in for four more hours."

"What about her home address?" Hawke asked.

Grady winced. "I can't give that out."

Sigga waved her badge again. "This says you can."

The registration clerk stared at the monitor under the registration desk and rattled off an address. Hawke didn't understand the words, but Sigga nodded.

They walked out to the parked car. Hawke settled onto the passenger seat and his stomach rumbled.

"We can get something to eat on the way to Tinna's," Sigga said.

"Sounds good." He buckled his seat belt and placed his hat in his lap.

After lunch, Sigga parked the car in a lot in front of

what she called Árbær neighborhood.

Hawke studied the long buildings that resembled motels in the states, except these buildings had immaculate trees and shrubs and small well-maintained patches of grass. Each apartment appeared to be two stories with a small patio in the back.

"There is the apartment. There's a car in the spot. She should be here," Sigga said.

"Do people rent these?" Hawke asked, curious at what the price would be compared to the one room with a bath he rented over a horse arena back home.

"Most of the apartments in this area have been purchased. Renting is unstable. You can be kicked out after a few months."

"Kicked out? Because they want to sell?"

"Or someone is willing to pay more rent." Sigga walked up to the door and knocked.

Hawke contemplated Sigga's words.

The door opened. "Hállo?" a woman in her thirties asked.

Sigga introduced them and asked if she was Tinna.

"Yes." Tinna studied them. "Why do you wish to talk to me?"

Hawke motioned to the inside. "We can explain inside."

The woman backed up, and they walked in, following her into a small sitting area.

"Do you live here alone?" he asked.

"Yes. I make enough at the hotel to manage on my own. I like it that way." Tinna sat on a chair, leaving the small couch for him and Sigga.

Sigga sat, he stood, holding his hat in his hands.

"Tinna, why did you slip a key under the door of

room two-nineteen on Wednesday night?" Hawke used a casual tone.

"How did you…" Tinna shook her head.

"Surveillance. The key, along with a note, was left on the registration desk. It said, 'borrowed this, please slip under door of room two-nineteen.' I didn't see any harm. And when the person in that room didn't ask about the key, I figured it had been arranged that would be how the key was returned."

"I don't suppose you still have the note?" Sigga asked.

"No. I wadded it up and tossed it in the waste basket." Tinna glanced at the two of them. "Am I in trouble?"

"No. We're just determining how the keys were returned to Mr. Largess." Hawke sighed. Another boulder in the investigation. They had to come up with a solid lead soon.

"Thank you for your time," Sigga said, standing.

Walking out to the car, Hawke said, "We need surveillance tapes of the registration counter."

"I'll start the paperwork rolling when I get back to the station. Where do you want to go?"

Hawke didn't know which direction to try next. "The station. If Böðvarsson hasn't heard back from the people I gave him this morning, I'll make some calls."

Hawke walked into the detective inspector's office. The man held up a hand as he talked on the phone. Hawke took a seat and waited.

Ending the call, Böðvarsson tapped a pen on the pad he'd been writing on. "That was the airport. Billy Weston entered Iceland a week ago. His return flight is not until next week. I have been on the phone calling all hotels. He is not staying at a hotel."

"He is here and has been here." Hawke twirled his Stetson in his hands. "There's a chance he followed our victim and when he saw him alone did what he came here to do."

"Or he is just here on vacation." Böðvarsson studied him. "You don't know for sure that Billy is the one who killed Nonni."

"From everything I've found, he is the only person who had a problem with Nonni. Back home, we'd call Nonni an altar boy or a goody-goody. Other than partying with his friends and keeping them off drugs, which is admirable, he doesn't have any reason for anyone in this country to want him dead."

"We still haven't ruled out random killing." Böðvarsson put down the pen and picked up a file.

"You may not, but the tracks I followed back to the parking lot weren't made by someone who was scared, paranoid, or worried about what they'd just done. The stride was even and purposeful. That to me means it was a premeditated killing." He'd had to voice a similar argument some years ago to get his superior to take another look at a homicide. They had, and eventually gathered enough information to put the woman's boyfriend in jail.

"I have two officers working on tracking down where he could be staying."

"Do you have a photo of him?" Hawke wasn't waiting around for what could take days. He'd enlist Nonni's friends to take him to all the bars.

"What are you planning?"

"I'd like to know what he looks like. That way

when I find him, I can talk to him, learn where he is staying, and let you know."

Böðvarsson studied him. "That's all you plan to do?"

"I might ask him why he's here." That wasn't lying. He would ask the man why he was in Iceland.

"I'm not sure about this. If I show you the photo, you promise you will take Sigga with you on your hunt?"

He didn't want the woman along. "What if he recognizes her as someone from the conference? I wouldn't get as much information out of him."

Böðvarsson handed a photocopy of a photo across the desk.

Hawke pulled out his phone and took a picture of the photo. "Thanks."

He stood, walking to the door.

"Don't do anything that will cause embarrassment to this country or my officers," Böðvarsson said.

"I won't. You have my word on that."

Chapter Thirteen

It was dark, noisy, and bodies bumped and gyrated in the flashing lights of the dance floor. Hawke felt out of his element. Ásta, Bragi, and Katrín were grinning and dancing with everyone who came along and asked. They appeared to know at least half of the people at the establishment. He'd told them he was looking for someone and showed them the photo.

This was the third place they'd checked out. He was ready to call it a night and go home. He'd sipped on a beer at each place, never finishing it. All he wanted was to go to his quiet room and relax.

Katrín danced back to the table. "I think I saw the person."

Hawke sat up straight and studied her animated face. "Where?"

"He's over there with people I know. Want me to introduce you?" She held out a hand.

He was old enough to be her father and wondered how she would introduce him. "Sure." He grasped Katrín's hand and followed her through the undulating bodies.

She stopped at a table with two couples. He recognized Billy Weston immediately. Katrín had indeed found the man he was looking for. Weston had an arm around a busty brunette who looked as if she were about to pass out.

Katrín faced the other couple. "Solla and Jón, this is my friend Hawke."

They studied him and shook hands.

"Hello," Jón said. "These are our friends, Valdís and Billy."

"Billy?" Hawke said. "You must be American or English?"

The man nodded. "American. You sound American, too."

"Yeah. Oregon." He settled Katrín on the chair next to Solla and pulled a chair from another table over and sat. "Where are you from?"

"Philly." The man said it with pride.

"Never been there. I hear it has a lot of history." Hawke ordered a drink for him and Katrín when the waitress came around. The waitress raised an eyebrow. Katrín said something in Icelandic and the woman smiled before heading the other direction.

"What was that about?" Hawke asked the young woman.

"We," she pointed to Solla and Valdís, "women in Iceland don't let men buy our drinks."

He stared at her. "It's courteous."

"No, it means you will expect something and you

may not be the man we wish to end the night with." She leaned towards him. "And you are much too old for me."

Hawke stared at her. She knew he wasn't here to pick up anyone, why would him buying her drink matter? Either she was pulling his leg or she was pretending he had that idea to keep Billy and the others not knowing his real reason for dropping down at their table.

Katrín ignored him, visiting with the couple next to her in Icelandic.

"She got you there," Billy said. "But I'm not a woman and I'm not Icelandic." Billy eyed Hawke's drink and then his own empty glass.

Hawke waved the waitress down and bought a drink for Billy.

When the drinks arrived, Billy toasted him.

"Are you vacationing or working here?" Hawke asked.

"Vacation." The man didn't seem to be leery of the questions. "You?"

"I'm here for a SAR conference."

Billy stared at him. "SAR?" The tone said he knew the answer.

"Search and Rescue. I'm a tracker. Taught a class on that the other day." Hawke held the beer up to his lips as he studied the man.

"Heard there was an accident at the conference." Again, the non-committal tone with a drop of curiosity.

"The person we were tracking was murdered," Hawke said it bluntly as he peered into the man's eyes.

"How unfortunate for him, and you, I guess." Weston took a drink and stood, drawing the woman next to him to her feet. "Let's dance."

Hawke had a feeling the man was going to leave, but he couldn't apprehend him. The two staggered onto the dance floor and disappeared among the moving bodies.

"Where is Billy staying?" he asked the two remaining at the table.

Solla shrugged. "We ran into him here. He offered us the use of the table and then he and Valdís decided to hook up."

Katrín held up her phone. "I can ask Valdís tomorrow. Solla gave me her phone number."

Hawke smiled at the young woman. "Good thinking. I'm going home now. Tell Bragi and Ásta I enjoyed hanging out with all of you tonight."

Katrín's grin dissolved. "We want to help find out who killed Nonni. He was a very good friend."

"And I appreciate your help. Talk to you tomorrow." Hawke walked out of the nightclub and into the foggy night air. He'd yet to see a clear night and stars. He inhaled the cold, damp air and started walking toward his hotel. While he'd picked his hotel to be near the conference center, it was also within walking distance of many of the downtown restaurants and clubs.

He entered his hotel.

"Mr. Hawke, you have mail." The young woman behind the registration desk held out a long business-like envelope.

Surprised anyone would leave him a letter, he walked over and plucked the envelope from her hand. He turned it over and over. The only marking was his name printed in block letters with blue ink.

"Thank you." He didn't open it. Instead, he entered the elevator, pushed the button, and continued turning the thing over and over until the door opened, and he stepped into the hall.

In his room, he pulled out his pocketknife and slit the top. Hawke pushed on the ends, causing the envelope to gap and show him what looked like an unfolded single piece of paper inside. He grasped it by a corner and pulled it out. In block letters written in the same blue ink as the envelope it read:

LOOK INTO SIGGA EIRÍKSDÓTTIR'S MEN

Hawke dropped the paper back into the envelope and set both on the counter under the television. What did Sigga's love life have to do with the murder? He remembered how she'd been upset with Nonni being tracked. She'd wanted that opportunity. What could that have had to do with his death and her men?

The promiscuousness of the culture in this country was alien to him. When Leonard had mentioned it, he'd thought it was only the young people who fell into bed together, knowing very little about the other person. But after his visits to the various nightclubs and bars, he'd noticed all ages leaving in pairs.

He prepared for bed, tossing around the best way to find out about the Chief Inspector's men. Ask Largess? Ask Böðvarsson? He should take the note to forensics to be checked for prints. Or the very least to try and figure out where the note came from.

Hawke picked up the phone in his room and dialed the registration desk.

"Hello?" the young woman answered.

"This is Hawke in room three-fourteen. Did you see who left that envelope for me?" He knew it was a long shot but worth trying.

"No. I was called to a room and when I returned it was sitting on the counter."

"Do you have a surveillance camera in the lobby?" Again, a long shot given how clever the person was slipping the key under Largess's door. If it was the same person, there wouldn't be any sign of them. Which would mean it was the killer trying to throw him off. But if they did catch someone, then it could be Sigga was a person of interest and should be taken off the case.

Saturday morning.

Hawke hurried and dressed. They only had today and tomorrow to catch whoever did this, if it was a person attending the conference. Monday the conference attendees would be scattering back to their homes in other countries.

He shoved the envelope into his pack. Riding the elevator to the lobby, he called Böðvarsson.

"I have evidence that needs to be taken into consideration," he said. "I'll bring it to the police station."

"What evidence?" The detective's tone said he was skeptical. "Did you discover where Billy Weston is staying?"

"Not yet. But I'll know soon. This is different. I'm catching a cab and will meet you at your office." Hawke stepped out of the elevator and walked to the desk. "Could you call a ride for me?"

"Where do you wish to go?" the woman at the desk was new.

"The police station."

She studied him before picking up the phone and talking into it. Replacing the phone, she said, "You will have a ride in five minutes."

"Thank you." He walked out the double doors and stood in front of the hotel, waiting for his ride. A glance at his watch revealed it was too early to ask Katrín if she'd come up with where Billy was staying.

A car pulled up to the curb. The window rolled down. "You going to the police station?"

"Yes." Hawke grabbed the back passenger door and slid in.

The driver tried to make conversation but gave up when Hawke ignored his questions.

At the police station, Hawke paid the driver and entered the building. From his previous trips, he knew where to find Böðvarsson. Walking down the hall, his name was called out. Before he spun around, he knew who it was and wondered why she was here so early.

"Sigga. Didn't expect to see you here this morning." Hawke remained glued to the spot.

"If, like you think, we need to get this solved before the conference is over, I figured I needed to be here rather than taking in a class." She strode down the hall toward him. "Ari said you were coming in."

Hawke groaned inwardly and motioned for her to lead the way to the detective's office.

In the office, he noticed a large pile of files on the man's desk. Böðvarsson motioned for them both to take a seat.

"Are all of those files for Nonni's case?" Hawke asked, avoiding the reason he came here.

The detective put his hand on the stack. "Not all of them. I did pull files on people who have had a grudge with Einar. Thought we might try that angle since we aren't getting anywhere with people who were angry with Nonni."

"We know Billy Weston had a beef with him. And he is here. When I brought up I was here for the SAR conference, he became cautious. He even said he'd heard we'd found a body." Hawke thought back to the conversation. "He said it almost with a touch of pride. I think he is our best suspect at the moment."

"Is that what you wanted to tell me this morning?" Böðvarsson asked.

Hawke slid a sideways glance at Sigga and peered at the detective. "I had a letter dropped off at my hotel last night." He pulled the envelope out of his pack and slid it across the desk. "I only touched the top right corner of the note."

Böðvarsson opened the letter by squeezing the ends as Hawke had done the night before. He grasped the note the same way and pulled it out. He read the line and his gaze shot to Sigga.

"What?" she asked, rising out of the chair.

Böðvarsson knew the woman better than he did. He'd let the detective inspector handle this as he saw fit.

"This note suggests Hawke look into the men in your life." Böðvarsson's tone had an inflection of reprimand in it.

Sigga stared at the detective and slowly melted into the chair. "I see."

"Did you sleep with Largess to get your hands on his keys?" Hawke asked, trying to keep his distaste for her sleeping around out of his voice. "And who were you sleeping with that you asked someone to kill

Nonni?"

"I didn't do any of that!" She glared at him.

"Why would someone suggest your sleeping around had anything to do with Nonni's death?" Böðvarsson asked, more diplomatic than Hawke.

Her face turned red. She didn't look at either of them.

"You weren't fooling around with Nonni, were you?" Hawke would lose his respect for the woman and the young man if that were true. She was nearly twenty years older than the murder victim.

"No. He was a boy. A boy who didn't understand that sometimes a marriage needs to be spiced up." She glanced at Böðvarsson and then back at her hands in her lap.

"You and Einar?" the detective asked.

"When? Did Nonni know and he threatened to tell his mother?" Hawke could see the young man everyone admired for his truthfulness not withholding his father's affair. "Was that why you had him killed?"

"I didn't have him killed!" Her hands clenched and she stared daggers at him. "Yes, he threatened to tell his mother. But I would never kill him for that or any reason. It was Einar's problem, not mine."

Hawke latched onto, 'Einar's problem.' He glanced at Böðvarsson. "You know the family better than I do. Would Einar wish to keep his affair quiet from his wife?"

The detective ran a hand over his face. "I thought I knew the man, but he has been acting out of character since Nonni's death."

"So, we can't rule out the father," Hawke said.

"No. Einar would never end his son's life. He

nearly fell apart after Halldór's death." Sigga sat up straight and searched their faces.

"Who would he be more likely to let go? His wife or his son?" Hawke asked. Would the man be so desperate to keep his wife that he'd kill a son?

His phone buzzed. Katrín.

"Hello?"

"Hawke, Valdís sent me the address for the man last night. Do you wish us to go talk to him?"

"No. The address is all I need. You and your friends need to stay away from him." He had a thought. "Could you ask Ásta if she would have time to have lunch with me today? I have questions I would like to ask her."

"I will tell her. Where would you like to meet?" Katrín's tone sounded as if she were used to making appointments.

"I'll text her. Text me the address."

"I will."

He hung up and his phone dinged. He held the phone out to the detective. "This is where we will find Billy Weston."

The man stood. His gaze landed on Sigga. "I suggest you go with us, since we don't want you reporting what we know to Einar."

"And take her phone," Hawke added.

Böðvarsson held out his hand.

Sigga glared at Hawke and handed her phone over to the detective.

Chapter Fourteen

The house Böðvarsson parked in front of was compact and on a bit of a hill. Hawke glanced at the number of the house on his phone. They were the same. He had expected to see apartments like Tinna had lived in.

"He's renting a house? That has to be expensive," Hawke said, as Böðvarsson and Sigga exited the vehicle.

"He's renting the basement. The kj after the number is short for *kjallari*, which means basement." Böðvarsson walked to the front door and knocked.

"Hállo?" a man in his sixties answered the door.

The detective talked to the man in Icelandic. The man waved to the side of the house and after a quick exchange of good-byes, Sigga and Böðvarsson, with Hawke in tow, walked to the side of the house.

"It was as I thought. Billy is renting the basement

apartment for two weeks. He has been here a week, staying out late at night and coming in early in the morning. But the man says he is quiet when he is here and he is respectful." Böðvarsson stopped at the door with entry to the basement and knocked.

"This may be too early for him to rise and shine," Hawke said, standing behind the other two. He didn't want the man seeing him and not opening the door.

The door opened and the woman, Valdís, stood in the opening. "Yes?"

"Is Billy here?" Böðvarsson asked.

"Yes. He is still sleeping. You can come back." She started to shut the door.

"We can't come back later." To his credit, Böðvarsson stepped toward the woman.

She backed into the apartment. Sigga followed the detective, and Hawke walked in and closed the door.

From the shape Valdís had been in the night before, Hawke doubted she would remember him.

"Billy doesn't like being woke up before noon," the woman insisted.

"We don't have time to wait till noon," Hawke said, scanning the small area and figuring out where the bedroom was located. He took a step that direction.

Böðvarsson put out an arm. "Sigga stay with her." He walked ahead of Hawke toward the door that had to be the bedroom.

Inside the room, they found a double bed with sheets and blankets wadded in piles. Billy was spread out across the bed on his belly. His mouth hung open. Low snoring vibrated the air.

"Billy Weston?" Böðvarsson questioned loudly.

The man didn't move.

Hawke walked through the room to the next door. The bathroom was cramped, but it had a cup. He filled the vessel with water, walked into the bedroom, and threw it on the sleeping man.

"What the fuck!" Billy shot to his hands and knees. "Valdís, why—" His mouth clamped shut as his gaze locked onto Hawke and the detective.

"Billy Weston?" Böðvarsson asked again, this time not as loud.

"Yeah. Who are you?" A hostile glare narrowed Weston's eyes as his gaze lingered on Hawke.

"I'm Detective Inspector Ari Böðvarsson of the Reykjavik Police. We'd like to ask you a few questions." Böðvarsson grabbed the only chair in the room, dumped the clothing off of it, and sat, facing the bed.

"Who is he?" Weston sat up, revealing he had nothing but the sheet on. He grabbed a handful of the bedding, pulling it over his lap.

"I'm Oregon State Trooper Hawke."

"Why are you here?" He swung his arm back and forth between them. "Both of you?"

Hawke refrained from jumping in. This was Böðvarsson's jurisdiction, not his.

"We were wondering the same about you?" the detective asked.

Weston stared at Böðvarsson like he'd just sprouted Viking horns. "Me? I'm here on vacation. Why else would I be here?"

Böðvarsson shrugged. "Perhaps to settle a score?"

"Settle a score? I don't have any—" He stopped and stared at Hawke. "You think I killed the guy who drowned in a mud pool?"

"You did have an altercation with him four years ago at the conference that is happening right now." Hawke took off his hat, shoved his hair back with the other hand, and replaced his hat. "Kind of makes one wonder…"

"That guy was a nerd. He could have told my dad quietly what he thought, but he blabbed it to everyone who would listen and then some. He deserved the beating I gave him four years ago." Weston's hands clenched and unclenched.

"But that wasn't enough. You waited. Came back when things seemed to have simmered down and waited for your chance for retribution." Hawke glanced at Böðvarsson. He didn't seem to care that Hawke was doing all the talking.

"I didn't need retribution. Dad is suing the conference. Money is better than boiling someone up." Weston grinned smugly.

"How do you know he was boiled?" Böðvarsson asked.

"Because I saw it on the news. You can't blame this on me. I didn't do it." Weston was starting to get antsy.

"Where were you Wednesday afternoon?" Hawke asked.

"Driving around."

"Where were you driving?" the detective asked.

"I don't know. Just driving. There isn't a law against driving."

"Do you have a rental car?" Hawke asked.

"No, I borrowed one." The man started sweating. "I don't remember the girl's name. I met her Tuesday night at a bar, mentioned I wanted to drive around and see more of the country. She spent the night and I drove her to work and used her car."

Hawke rolled his eyes. He'd never been that stupid even in his teens.

"What bar and where did she work?" Böðvarsson had a notepad in his left hand and a pen in his right.

"I met her at the bar at Harpa," Weston said.

Hawke took a step forward. "Nonni and his friends were in that bar that night. You sure you didn't recognize him and past anger resurfaced?"

"I didn't see Nonni or anyone else I recognized."

"Why did you go to the place where the conference was being held?" Böðvarsson asked.

Weston whipped his gaze to the detective. "I didn't know the conference was there. Four years ago it was someplace else."

Hawke stared at Weston. "You didn't see the banner and the signs welcoming the attendees to the SAR conference?"

Weston stared back at him, his mouth pinched shut.

Looked like he needed to try a different tactic. "Why did you come to Iceland now? There are other times during the year that would be better for a vacation." Hawke could only think of one reason the man came now, during the conference—to harm Nonni.

"It was cheaper now. Off-season and all."

"Why did you want to come here?" Böðvarsson had his pen poised over the notepad, which reminded Hawke that Weston had yet to answer the question of where the girl worked.

"When I was here during the conference, I liked the people and wanted to see more of the country. I saved up to get here now. I'm not going to let you ruin my trip."

"What was the girl's name and where did she work?" Hawke pushed.

"Asa, Ashta, I don't know. She worked at an office in the government building." He ran a hand over the back of his neck. "I didn't know I needed to keep a list of the women I met here."

Hawke's head whipped up at the name that sounded like Nonni's girlfriend. But she had been with Nonni that night. Or had she? He'd seen them early in the evening. Had Billy won her away from Nonni? In which case, Nonni would have wanted revenge, not Weston.

"We will check this out with, did you say Ásta?" Böðvarsson asked.

"That sounds right," Weston said. "I don't know which office she works in. She has reddish hair that's long and curly. Freckles and a funny laugh. She also has a birthmark on the inside of her thigh." The man's grin twisted into a goofy smirk.

Böðvarsson's pen punctuated the last thing he wrote and he stood. "We may have more questions for you."

Hawke had plenty but this wasn't his country or his jurisdiction. He did breathe a sigh of relief. The description of the woman wasn't close to the Ásta he knew as Nonni's girlfriend.

"Did you get anything out of the woman?" Hawke asked Sigga as Böðvarsson drove them to the government building.

"She met up with Billy last night. Thought he was a lot of fun and was hanging around to show him the

sights, go to dinner, and hook up again tonight."
Sigga's tone reflected she was still unhappy with him
believing she had anything to do with Nonni's death.

Until he was certain she and a possible lover, like
Largess, whose car had been at the parking lot, hadn't
worked together to kill Nonni, he wasn't going to trust
her completely. The car in the parking lot after the body
was found still bothered Hawke. If the killer walked to
the parking lot ahead of him, but didn't leave in the
rental car, until after Hawke had written down the
license plates, had they still been walking around,
mingling with others to take suspicion off? He knew
Sigga hadn't driven the car there, she had been on the
bus and she had ridden back to town with him and
Böðvarsson. Who drove the car there and who brought
it back?

Böðvarsson stopped in a parking lot in front and to
the side of a long white older building that Hawke had
walked past several times while following Nonni's
friends from bar to bar.

"This is a government building?" He stepped out of
the car and studied the architecture.

"It is now. Before it was a prison." Böðvarsson
walked to the entrance. Inside, he showed his
identification and asked to see Ásta.

"Last name? We have three who work in this
building," the woman at the information counter said.

"She has red curly hair and freckles." Hawke left
off the other distinguishing mark, figuring the woman
in her sixties hadn't had the pleasure of seeing Ásta's
inner thigh.

"I'll give her a call. Is she in trouble?" The woman
picked up the phone.

"We just have some questions for her," Böðvarsson said, smiling.

The woman nodded, spoke into the phone, and smiled at them. "She'll be right down."

They moved to a small area with a few chairs and stood, waiting.

A robust young woman with long curly red hair and freckles, sauntered down the hall toward them. She smiled and held out a hand when she stood in front of Sigga.

Böðvarsson cleared his throat and extended his hand. "Ari Böðvarsson, from the CID."

Ásta shook his hand and glanced at Hawke. She started speaking in Icelandic.

Hawke held up his hand. "Could you speak in English, please."

"I asked what you wanted to see me about?" She smiled at him and studied Böðvarsson.

"Were you at the Bergmál on Tuesday night?" the detective asked.

"Yes. I'm a big girl. I can go out for a drink on a work night." She winked at Hawke.

"Did you meet anyone?" Böðvarsson asked.

Her grin grew larger and her eyes sparkled. "I did. He was American. Very talented." She glanced at Sigga. "If you know what I mean."

"Did you spend the night with him and lend him your car the next day?" Hawke wasn't interested in the woman's love life.

"I did both. He wanted to do some sightseeing and I didn't need the car while I was cooped up in here." She glanced at Sigga again. "Besides, I wanted him to be available another night. You know, owing me a favor."

"Did he say where he'd gone that day?" Böðvarsson asked.

"I think he traveled south. He talked about the two of us going north this weekend."

Hawke wondered if she realized he'd picked up another woman last night. "Where south? Any place in particular?"

"Why are you asking all of these questions about Billy?" She no longer grinned. Her eyes had narrowed and she studied them with suspicion.

"We're looking into the homicide that happened near Lake Kleifarvatn," Böðvarsson said.

Her eyes widened. "You think Billy had something to do with that? No! I don't believe it. He is kind and funny. He couldn't kill someone."

"Could we look inside your car?" Böðvarsson asked.

"I'll have to get my keys. But I'm telling you. He wouldn't do something like that." She hurried back down the hall.

"What do you think?" Böðvarsson asked.

Sigga shook her head. "She wouldn't be the first woman to think a man she hooked up with was a saint."

Hawke studied the woman and said to the detective, "He went south. The lake is south and he had a motive. But why was Largess's car taken if Weston had access to Ásta's car?"

"That's why we are going to check the miles it has been driven since its last trip to a mechanic." Böðvarsson stood by the door waiting for the woman to return.

Chapter Fifteen

After looking all through the car and not finding anything out of the ordinary, Böðvarsson wrote down the miles, asked Ásta where she lived and who worked on her car, and they drove back to the police station.

Hawke sat in Böðvarsson's office making a list while the detective found some officers to decipher the information he'd written down about the car.

Sigga sat in a corner. She was still sulking. "What are you doing?" she asked.

"Making a list of what we don't know."

"Which is everything." She sighed. "I know I didn't kill him. You can take me off your list."

He studied her. She appeared truthful if not a bit subdued.

Böðvarsson entered the office. "The surveillance tapes arrived. From the Marina Hotel and the Center Hotel."

Hawke sat up. "Are they in the same room where I watched them before?"

"Yes. We are still trying to find information on Wanza and her mother. Though I doubt it has anything to do with our homicide." Böðvarsson sat down behind his desk. "I have to catch up on some paperwork."

Hawke stood. "I'll be looking at surveillance tape." He didn't wait to hear what Sigga would be assigned.

The room he sat in the previous day had the same young woman in charge of the technology. She had the Marina Hotel tape ready for him to view.

He stared at the tape, stopping and re-watching every time someone stepped up to the desk to see if they left the keys and note. It would help a lot if he had an idea of what time the keys had been dropped off. He knew when they were taken up to the rock climber's room. The staff would have returned the keys shortly after receiving them, would be his guess.

Hawke fast forwarded the tape to half an hour before Tinna slipped the keys under the door.

The tape showed her leaving the counter. Someone, in a big fluffy coat with a fur-lined hood, walked up to the desk, placed the key and note down and walked out with their head down. There wasn't a clear image of the person's face. He replayed the tape over and over trying to determine if it was a woman or a man. The hands had on gloves, no skin showed anywhere. The fur trimmed hat hid the face. The shoulders could have been broad or slender. The coat was so fluffy it was hard to distinguish if the person was slender or overweight. Even the waterproof pants gave no clue to the size or gender of the person. The hiking shoes. Maybe.

Hawke caught the young officer's attention.

"Could you get me a blown up shot of this person and their shoes, please."

She popped that tape out of the machine.

"And could you hand me the other tape?"

She handed the Center Hotel tape to him and wandered over to another machine in the room.

Hawke inserted the tape and found the time stamp for noon yesterday. He didn't have a clue when the letter had been delivered since he'd been out running around all day.

The door opened.

"You want some lunch?" Böðvarsson asked.

"Yeah, I'll get something when I find—" There was the same person entering the Center as had left the key. "There. The same person who left the key at the Marina Hotel."

Böðvarsson leaned down, staring at the monitor. "Not much to go on. They are dressed as if it were winter. We haven't been that cold. You would think someone would have noticed them."

Hawke continued to watch the video. The person walked in, placed the envelope on the counter with gloved hands and turned away from the camera, walking out. In both instances, it was as if the person had known where the surveillance cameras were and turned the opposite direction to keep from getting a photo of them.

It had to be someone local to know that. Or this person was working with someone else. Frustration rippled through Hawke. "Damn!" He shoved back from the monitor. "There has to be some way to catch this person. He is either the murderer or is helping the murderer."

"Do those clothes look local?" Hawke knew that was a long shot. Was the person local or had someone here for the conference purchased them.

"I'll get an officer to look these photos over and see if they can determine that. The clothes look new to me." Böðvarsson pointed to the monitor. "Except the shoes. Those look worn."

"They look familiar too." Hawke leaned back toward the monitor, studying the shoes.

Böðvarsson slapped him on the shoulder. "Let's get something to eat."

Hawke shoved away from the monitor and said to the technician, "Take a print of this person. too. I'll collect them after I eat."

"And make copies," the detective added.

During lunch, Böðvarsson asked Hawke a million questions about his life and job. While he was happy to answer the questions, in the back of his mind Hawke was trying to piece together what little information they had so far.

"I will bring my family to Oregon some day and look for you," Böðvarsson said as he parked behind the police station.

"Let me know and I'll get time off to show you around." Hawke stepped out of the car and walked to the back door of the building.

A man in his forties sat in a chair by the detective's office.

"Detective Inspector, this man would like to talk to you." An officer hurried out of the room next to Böðvarsson's.

Böðvarsson walked over to the man. "Why did you

wish to speak with me?"

"You are the one looking into the death at Krýsuvík?" the man asked.

"Yes. What do you know about the death?" Böðvarsson motioned for the man to enter his office.

Hawke kept on their heels to not miss a word.

The detective settled the man in a chair and moved to his seat behind the desk.

Hawke closed the door and sat in the only other chair.

"I thought it was odd when it happened, but after talking it over with my wife, she says, I should say something." The man wrung a stocking cap in his hands.

"What was odd?" Böðvarsson asked.

"Wednesday, I picked up a person at Harpa. He or she kept their face hid behind a fur-lined hood on the coat."

The hair on the back of Hawke's neck tingled. He wanted to ask questions, but refrained. The detective knew best how to handle a fellow countryman.

"What about this person? Did the voice sound like a man or a woman?"

"I couldn't tell. Husky enough to be a man but it could have been a woman."

"What did they want?"

"They asked me to take them to the parking lot at Krýsuvík. I asked why they needed to go there, it was dark and they wouldn't be able to see anything. They said their car had broken down and they had the part to fix it." He stared at Böðvarsson and then Hawke. "I told them to wait until morning, but they insisted they must go tonight." He shook his head. "I tried to talk on the drive, but the person kept their head turned, looking out the side window and didn't reply."

"What happened when you arrived at the parking lot?" Hawke asked.

"They handed me money and got out, keeping their face turned away. I called out, 'Sure you don't want me to wait in case the part doesn't work?' The person just walked away."

"When was this?" Böðvarsson asked.

"I picked the person up around eight. That was the other strange thing. Why would they want to be left out there after dark?"

"Were there any cars in the parking lot?" Hawke asked.

"Yes. Just one." The taxi driver studied Böðvarsson.

"What type of car was it?" Böðvarsson asked.

"A smaller car than my taxi. In the dark, I am unsure of the color. Perhaps blue, maybe black? Is that helpful?"

"Yes. Thank you for coming in. Can I get your name, address, and phone number?"

While the man recited his information, Hawke ran through the events of the day after finding the body. Had the killer ridden the bus back to Harpa and then went back to pick up the car? But who? And why weren't they noticed if they hadn't ridden the bus out? He was missing something. Neither he nor Sigga were on the bus back to town. When he'd interviewed the others, no one said anything about someone new riding back with them.

There hadn't been any time for someone who rode out with them to get ahead, knock Nonni in the head and dump him in the mud pot, and get back to the group.

The man left and Böðvarsson tapped his pen on his desk. "That has to be the person who used the rental car."

"Same clothing as the person who left the keys and the note for me." Hawke wasn't sure where to look next. "We don't know if it's male or female, what nationality—" He sat up. "We didn't ask the taxi driver if the person spoke in English or Icelandic or if they had an accent."

Böðvarsson picked up his phone and dialed.

"Dagur, this is Ari Böðvarsson. The person you picked up at Harpa, you said you couldn't tell if it was a man or a woman." He listened. "Did they speak in English or Icelandic?" He listened. "Did the person have an accent of any kind?" Böðvarsson's head nodded. "I see. Thank you. Yes. If you think of anything else, give me a call."

"What did he say?" Hawke asked, leaning forward in his chair.

Böðvarsson replaced the phone and leaned back in his chair. "He said it sounded British."

Hawke sat forward. "That still doesn't rule out Billy Weston. His Philly accent might sound British to someone here. I'll have a talk with Reggie Carlton. He's been coming here for years. He brought a daughter with him last conference. But he was on the bus there and back. I saw him. Hopefully, Carlton can tell me who else is here from that area or if he saw Billy Weston on the bus."

"But why did he use the young woman's car if he had the rental?" Böðvarsson asked.

"To throw us off. If he's been planning this for four years, he'd have it all figured out down to every detail."

"That's a long time to get things right. I'll have my officers try to track down the coat the person in the surveillance tape is wearing." Böðvarsson's phone rang.

Hawke used that as his cue to leave. Out in the lobby he asked for a ride to the Harpa. Once he was settled in the police car, he sank into his thoughts, ignoring the officer pointing out sights like a tour guide.

Chapter Sixteen

At the Harpa, Hawke thanked the officer for the ride and stood on the sidewalk, studying where people stood to catch buses and taxis. He walked over to the line that appeared to be waiting for a ride at a stand that explained the bus routes and to stand here for taxis. Scanning the surrounding area for a traffic or surveillance camera, he didn't see one. A building like this should have surveillance cameras. He'd have Böðvarsson ask about it. If there were cameras, it should show who was picked up by the taxi driver.

What bothered him the most was the fact the person had to have been on the bus back from their tracking seminar. It had to be someone in the workshop. He'd ask the woman in the base of operations room to print out a list of the people who'd signed up for his class.

He walked into the beautiful glass building. It

reminded him of his mother's beadwork. The colored honey-comb shaped glass resembled an intricate pattern that could be found on Indian regalia and items that were made for family members and to sell.

He climbed the stairs to the second floor and entered the base of operations room. He wasn't surprised to see Einar sitting at a desk, staring at a computer monitor. He was surprised to see the man was alone. A good time to ask Einar about his affair with Sigga.

Hawke grabbed a chair and dragged it over to where Einar sat.

"Hawke, what are you doing here? Did you find out who killed my son?" Einar sat up straighter.

"No, not yet. But we are gathering more leads." Hawke paused and glanced at the monitor with photos of Nonni swirling in and out of the screen. "We discovered you and Sigga were having an affair."

The man's face turned crimson, even his ears. "That has nothing to do with my son's death!"

"Are you sure? Did Nonni threaten to tell your wife—his mother—about the affair? Maybe Sigga didn't want it aired that she was sleeping with you, the coordinator of the conference? Maybe you didn't want your wife to find out?"

"This is all crazy! Neither I nor Sigga would hurt Nonni."

Quietly, Hawke said, "But you did by sleeping together."

Einar dropped his face into his hands and sobbed.

Hawke wasn't good with emotions, his own or anyone else's. He waited for the man to pull himself together, hoping no one came in.

Finally, Einar snuffled, wiped his hands over his face and peered at him through bloodshot eyes. "I only slept with her during the last conference. I was at a vulnerable state with the Weston legal action." He shook his head. "It started with me just finding someone who would listen in the bar. Next thing I knew, we were in her room and I found myself there every night during the conference." Einar stared straight into Hawke's eyes. "It was only during the conference. We have not been together since."

Hawke raised his hands. "Okay, but we had to get that out of the way. Has the legal action with the Westons finalized?"

"No. When a legal battle is being fought from such distance it is harder to complete and expensive for the Westons."

"I can imagine. Was what Nonni said so defaming that it is worth it to them to spend the money and sue?" Hawke had never understood grown people going to court over name calling. He'd always found either fighting it out or ignoring it worked.

"No, he was sticking up for the people who could have been badly hurt or killed due to Calvin's negligence. They will not win. My lawyer told me last week that they are bluffing, saying they have new evidence to prove how much Nonni's words had hurt Calvin's job." Einar shook his head. "Now I do not see how it matters. Nonni is gone. They could not do any more to hurt me." His jowls sagged and his eyes pooled unshed tears.

"Perhaps Nonni's death was their way of getting even and not losing any more money?" He liked Billy Weston for the murder. He just had to prove it.

The tech woman walked in. Her gaze landed on the two of them and she hurried to her seat at the computer.

"Could you give me a print out of the people who signed up for my tracking class, please?" He stood and crossed to where the woman sat.

She tapped keys and the screen popped up class titles. She clicked on his, it opened, and a printer whirred to the left.

"I'll get it." He walked to the printer and pulled the page out of the machine. A quick glance and his eyes landed on Reggie Carlton. "Any chance you could tell me where Reggie Carlton is right now?"

The woman typed and a new screen popped up. She said, "He's in the Ríma room." She glanced up at him. "They should be getting out in about fifteen minutes."

"Thank you."

Hawke left the room, more determined than ever to pin the murder on Billy. But he was thorough and would visit with Carlton to make sure there wasn't a person with a British accent who hadn't been a fan of Nonni's.

Conference attendees trickled out of the room in front of where Hawke stood waiting. He'd scanned the list of people who'd signed up for his class and while he wasn't sure what he was looking for, nothing jumped out at him.

"Hawke, why are you lurking in the halls?" Carlton asked, walking over to him.

He smiled. "Waiting for you."

"Me? Why would you want to talk to me?" Carlton continued walking. Hawke fell in step beside him.

"Do you have time for a cup of coffee?" Hawke followed the man to the elevators.

"Yes. We will have some privacy upstairs in the room where the buffet was the other night." They stepped into the elevator and Carlton pushed the button. "Have you had any luck finding out who killed Nonni?"

"We have some leads. That's what I wanted to talk to you about."

The elevator dinged and the door slid open. Carlton stepped out and walked to a serve yourself coffee bar.

After they filled cups and Carlton doctored his with cream and sugar, they sat at a table along the outside wall where they both had a nice view of the water and boats.

"Why do you need to talk to me?" Carlton set his cup on the table and studied Hawke.

"A cab driver, who we believe picked up the murderer, didn't get a look at the person to tell if it was a man or woman and he said he couldn't tell if it was a man, or a woman making their voice sound like a man, but he did notice a British accent." Hawke had to give the man credit, he didn't start arguing it couldn't be him. He thought about what Hawke said.

"So, you believe you are looking for someone with a British accent. Someone connected to the conference?"

"I have one other lead, but it is also connected to the conference in a way. I do think it has to be someone either attending the conference or working the conference who has a British accent or an accent that sounds British." Hawke sipped his coffee. "Sound like anyone you can think of?"

"Why are you asking me? Because I'm British?"

The man scowled and stirred his coffee.

"That and because you have been to this conference many times. You know more of the people involved than I do."

"Sigga would know more people." Carlton stared at him.

"But she isn't reliable."

Carlton laughed. "You discovered her dirty little secret. She was shagging Einar. It was a one off. Not sure what was happening at home, but whatever you say about Sigga, she is a good listener."

"She also has a hot temper when it comes to her boy toys." Hawke wondered if Carlton knew about Sigga's on and off relationship with Largess and if Carlton had needed a good listener over the years he came to the conference.

"Really? I hadn't noticed that. It could mean whoever is boiling her blood may be the one she doesn't want to lose?" Carlton raised his eyebrows as if questioning Hawke to dish what he knew.

"The reason I waited for you; can you think of anyone with a British accent you've run into here that you remember from past conferences who may have had a beef with Nonni?" Hawke glanced up as two people entered the room. The Tanakas. He leaned his head their direction. "I know they both speak broken English, but have you ever witnessed any altercations between them and Nonni?"

Carlton shook his head. "No. I think Riku had a thing for Nonni. And as far as I could tell, her father didn't mind."

Hawke made a note to ask Ásta and the other friends how they felt about Nonni making so many female friends. He could tell Ásta was grieving for Nonni but was it because he was dead or because she'd killed him? That was a grasp at anything that could have happened. Best to stick with what they knew. The person in the hooded coat, the taxi ride, and the return of the keys. They had to find something useful from the clues.

"There are several SAR officers from Scotland and Britain here. Only one, Major Rumford, has been here before. But I can't see him and Nonni not getting along. The man loves etiquette and rule followers and that was Nonni."

Carlton stirred his coffee.

Hawke realized it was a stall tactic while deciding what to say. He picked up his cup, sipped, and waited.

"Any chance you could tell me what you know? Perhaps I could be of some assistance?" Carlton picked up his cup as if to take a drink.

"At the moment, the fewer people who know what we do, the less likely the person is to feel as if we are drawing the net tighter." Hawke took a drink.

A hand tapped his back. He glanced over his shoulder. It was Riku.

"Mr. Hawke, my father would like to speak to you at our table." She didn't glance at Carlton.

"Okay." He smiled at the Brit and followed the young woman across the room to where her father sat. Hawke set down his cup, held out his hand to shake, and took a seat.

"Why did you want to talk to me?" he asked, without preamble.

"We, my daughter and I, have been talking. She has been going out every night with Nonni's friends and she hears things." He glanced at his daughter who sat on the man's left side.

"What kind of things do you hear? Are they speaking in English?"

She shook her head and her cheeks became pinker. "I have been learning Icelandic for my return trip. I wished to speak with Nonni." Her cheeks darkened even more and the tips of her ears also blushed.

"I see. You have been eavesdropping on their private conversations?" He didn't mean it to come out as a reprimand, but the young woman cowered a bit. "What have you heard?"

Her nose wrinkled and her eyes narrowed. "Ásta does not like me. She is glad I did not get to be with Nonni."

He nodded his head. There was jealousy. Would she have killed him to keep him from falling for Riku? Something to think about. "What else?"

"Sindri is taking acting lessons. He wishes to be next James Bond." She rolled her eyes. "And Nonni and his friends knew the man you were looking for, Billy, was in Iceland. They said something about a meeting. But then other people came by and they talked of other things." She stared at him. "I did good? I wish to help find who killed Nonni."

"You did very good. Thank you, Riku." Hawke pulled the notebook out of his day pack and began writing it all down. "You need to be careful and not let them know you are listening."

"I have warned her of this. She should not go out with them anymore. I do not want something happen to her." Mr. Tanaka put a hand on his daughter's arm.

Hawke peered into Riku's eyes. "I agree with your

father. What you have told me will help me enough to get to the truth. Stay away from the others. I, and I know Nonni, wouldn't want you to be hurt because of him."

Tears sparkled in the corners of her eyes. "I will stay with my father and not go out."

"Good. And I will let you both know when we have Nonni's murderer."

"*Arigatou gozaimasu,* Thank you." Mr. Tanaka stood and bowed. Riku bowed as well and they both walked out of the room.

Hawke felt as if someone were watching. He scanned the room and discovered Carlton, Sigga, and Einar at the door watching him.

Chapter Seventeen

Time was running out. Tomorrow would be Sunday and everyone, other than the people staying for the Snow Jeep tour would be leaving. And Dani would be arriving on Monday. He wanted this cleared up to not impose on her vacation.

Hawke called Böðvarsson.

"Did you get the surveillance tapes from around the Harpa area?" he asked as soon as the detective answered.

"Yes. The prosecutor understands the need to get this wrapped up before people scatter."

"Good. Can you send a car to pick me up at the Harpa? Also, I have some new information." He went on to tell Böðvarsson what Riku had told him.

"His friends? I don't think they would kill Nonni."

"Niether do I, but they all knew Billy Weston was here. They mentioned something about a meeting. I think that's enough to ask them to come in and talk with us."

Böðvarsson sighed. "I agree. I'll have an officer call and request they come in this afternoon."

"And send a car for me."

"Yes. I will send a car for you."

The connection went silent.

Hawke hurried out to the front of the Harpa. He didn't want to miss the police car picking him up and miss out on Nonni's friends being questioned.

Hawke sat in a room with Böðvarsson and Bragi. He had been the first of Nonni's friends to arrive at the police station.

"I don't understand why you think I would know anything about Nonni's death." The young man drew rings on the top of the table with a fingertip, keeping his gaze cast downward.

Böðvarsson nodded to Hawke.

"We've learned that Billy Weston and Nonni had a meeting. And that you and the rest of his friends knew about it."

Bragi's shoulders drooped. He slowly raised his gaze to Hawke's. "Nonni told us not to tell anyone. He was trying to make the problem between the Westons and his family go away. They, Nonni and his father, set up the place where Billy is staying."

Hawke slapped a hand on the table.

The young man jumped and leaned back.

"You all knew where he was staying, and yet, I had to wait until the next morning for Katrín to send me the address?" Hawke stood and paced back and forth. What kind of friends withheld information that would expose their friend's killer? "I'd told you that I believed his killer was here with the conference, that we had to catch him before everyone headed home." He sat back down. "You all knew who he was before I showed you the photo and asked you to help me find him." He glared at Bragi. "Did you take me to all the other bars, hoping I'd give up?"

"No! We didn't know which bar he was at."

"But you knew where he was staying!" Because he rarely lost his composure, Hawke stood up, waved to Böðvarsson to continue, and stepped out of the room. How could the group have been so stupid to not tell him the truth from the beginning? Nonni was dead, breaking a promise would help them find his killer. He paced up and down the hall until he was back in control and walked into the room.

Böðvarsson stood. "I'll have your statement printed out and will bring it in for you to sign." He put a hand on Hawke's shoulder. "You back in control?"

"Yeah." Hawke sat, crossed his arms, and leaned back in the chair, staring at Bragi.

The young man squirmed.

"Did Nonni and Billy meet on Wednesday?"

Bragi shrugged. "I'm not sure. I know they planned to meet up this week, but I don't know if it was Wednesday."

Böðvarsson walked back in with a sheet of paper. "Read, make sure it is your words, and then sign." He nodded for Hawke to exit the room with him.

Out in the hall, the detective asked, "Can you keep it together for the rest of them?"

"Yeah. He blindsided me with already knowing where Billy was staying and withholding the information. I thought they wanted to help me. I think they've been mucking things up keeping Nonni's promises."

"I agree. They are very loyal to the victim, even if they could be helping a killer." Böðvarsson sighed and walked back in the room. He exited with Bragi. "Don't say a word to your friends about what we talked over when you leave."

The young man glanced at Hawke and nodded.

"Ready for the next one?" Böðvarsson asked.

"Yeah."

Sindri said the same about knowing Billy was in Iceland and that Nonni planned to meet with him to help out his father. He was given his statement to read and sign and moved along.

Hawke glared at Katrín, sitting across the table from him. "You pretended to not know where Billy was staying. Didn't you want to help find out who caused Nonni's death?"

She ducked her head. "We all promised Nonni we wouldn't tell anyone what he was doing."

"But he ended up dead. That promise should have become tell everyone so we could find out what happened to him." Hawke leaned back in his seat. "And it makes the four of you guilty of withholding evidence and hiding a suspect."

She inhaled and stared, wide-eyed at him.

"From now on when you are asked a question that pertains to Nonni's death, I want a straight answer, promises or not. Understood?"

"Yes." She batted her eyes and a tear trickled down one cheek.

Hawke hated tears, especially on women. But he

wasn't going to crumble to female shenanigans. This woman and her friends had to learn sometimes you had to break promises when lives were at stake.

"Was Ásta jealous of other women Nonni had for friends?"

Katrín lowered her lashes enough he couldn't see what was going on behind her eyes. She raised her chin and peered at him. "She is the jealous type. Even though she would go with other men, she didn't like Nonni to be with other women."

"How jealous is she? Would she rather kill Nonni than let another woman have him?"

She gasped. "Ásta didn't kill Nonni. She loved him."

"What you said doesn't sound like love. It sounds like control. Is Ásta controlling you, Bragi, and Sindri?" He'd picked up a nervous vibe from the group when Ásta talked. As if the others wanted to make sure they knew her thoughts on everything. As if they feared not pleasing her. "Is she why no one told me where to find Billy? Did she come up with the game of taking me to all the bars?"

Katrín nodded slightly. "She has always wanted to be the leader of our group, but we all looked up to Nonni. Now that he is gone, she has been telling us what we could say, who we could see."

Hawke nodded. "Thank you for coming in."

Böðvarsson went over getting the recording of her statement printed. He stood, saying he would bring it in for her to sign. Only this time, as he moved to the door, he motioned for Hawke to follow him out of the room.

"Where are you going with this knowledge about Ásta?" the detective asked.

"She may have made an alliance with Billy."

The detective nodded. "I'll have her put in the room next door, so she and Katrín do not pass in the hallway."

Hawke walked into the empty room. He rehashed the times he'd been with the group. The night he spoke with Nonni at the bar, Ásta had made it look as if she and Nonni were a couple. He wondered if Nonni had confided in her about his father and Sigga or if he hadn't trusted her with that information? But then why pull all of them into his attempt to appease the Westons if he didn't trust her?

The door opened. Ásta entered followed by Böðvarsson.

"Please have a seat. Information has come to us that we would like to ask you about," the detective said as they both sat.

She smiled at Hawke and sat casually in the chair. "What information is that?"

"That you took me on a wild goose chase trying to find Billy Weston when all four of you knew where he was." Hawke remained leaned back in his seat, his arms crossed, watching the young woman.

"We didn't take you on a chase. We didn't know which bar he was in." She stared him in the eyes.

Hawke returned her stare. "But you already knew where he was staying. When I showed you his photo and mentioned his name, why didn't any of you tell me what I'm just finding out today?"

"Nonni told us to keep his secret."

"The secret was void when Nonni ended up dead." Hawke leaned forward. "Did you help Billy kill Nonni?" It was blunt but it got a reaction.

"No! I would never help kill Nonni!" She shoved away from the table and acted as if she were going to stand.

"Not even to keep him from falling for someone else?" Hawke said it quietly.

Her body deflated against the back of the chair. "Katrín has loose lips. She thinks I am jealous, but I'm not. I only wanted what was best for Nonni."

"Was that you?" Hawke asked.

"No. I wasn't good for him, but I could keep him happy until the right person came along." She smiled. "I thought he was in love with Wanza. He always talked about how he sent her an email about school and he obsessed when she stopped replying to his emails. But then I saw him with Riku and I knew that was who he really loved. It showed on his face and in his eyes."

"What did you do about that?" Hawke asked.

She stared at him. "Nothing. I was going to wish them both well when we met at the bar on Wednesday night. But that never happened."

"And Billy Weston. How do you feel about him?" Hawke asked.

Ásta narrowed her eyes. "What do you mean?"

"Were you on his side or Nonni's?"

"That's a stupid question. I was on Nonni's side."

"But you like Billy?" Hawke studied her.

She licked her lips and shoved at her hair with a hand, stalling. "What has Billy said about me?"

There it was. She had been seeing Weston. "He told us you spent the night with him on Tuesday and he used your car on Wednesday."

"That's a lie! I wasn't with him then and he didn't have my car."

Böðvarsson cleared his throat. "That was a different Ásta."

She shot to her feet, spouting words that sounded profane in Icelandic. From Böðvarsson's chuckle Hawke had a feeling Billy would be safer with them than the scorned woman.

The detective said something and Ásta sat, clamping her mouth closed.

"From that outburst, I believe you do have feelings for Billy. Did you help him plan to kill Nonni?"

"No! He didn't kill Nonni and I didn't help him." She glanced from Böðvarsson to Hawke and back. "What time was Nonni killed?"

Böðvarsson gave her the estimated time.

She smiled. "Billy was with me."

"You just said you didn't lend him your car or spend the night with him the night before," Hawke was ready to catch her up in a lie.

"I didn't. He picked me up, we had lunch, and then drove back to his place for the afternoon." She smiled. "He couldn't have killed Nonni."

"Where did you have lunch and did anyone see you going to his place?" Böðvarsson asked.

She recited a restaurant and acknowledged the person who owned the house saw them when they were getting out of the car. He'd told Billy to park differently.

Hawke shoved to his feet and walked out of the room, leaving Böðvarsson to repeat about the recording and signing the form. He had a feeling their only suspect was going to be exonerated by the restaurant and his landlord.

Chapter Eighteen

The restaurant had remembered Ásta and Billy. It seemed they'd had a bit to drink while having lunch. The man who owned the house where Billy was staying also remembered when the two arrived. Billy had parked on the sidewalk and had been asked to remove the car from the sidewalk. The one person Hawke had believed had the only reason to want Nonni dead, had alibis.

Back at the police station, Böðvarsson poured a clear liquid into two small cups and handed one to Hawke. They sat in the detective's office.

"That did not go so well," the detective said, throwing back his drink.

Hawke sniffed the glass. "What is this?"

"Vodka. It will stimulate your brain. We have to figure out who else could have wanted Nonni dead." Böðvarsson sat at his desk and opened a folder.

"I need to look at the surveillance tapes." Hawke set the glass down, not attempting to drink.

"I have officers watching the tapes."

"They don't know what they are looking for." Hawke argued.

"They have the photo from the other surveillance tapes." Böðvarsson picked up the glass Hawke ignored and threw it back, giving a sigh. "We must go to what we know. What do we know?"

"Everyone liked the victim." Hawke pulled out the file he'd been keeping with his notes and the ones Böðvarsson had passed on to him.

"He was killed between eleven and one at the boiling mud pool south of Kleifarvatn and east of Krýsuvík," Böðvarsson added.

"By someone who must have followed him in Largess's rental car, then by foot, keeping out of sight until they came to the mud pool. There he was snuck up on and struck with a rock and fell or was shoved into the pool." Hawke glanced at the notes on the detective's desk. "Did forensics ever decide if he fell in or was put in the pool?"

Böðvarsson studied him. "Does that make a difference? Either way he ended up in the *leirhver*."

"If it was by accident that's one thing. But if the person who hit him, put him in the pool, that would mean they had a lot of hate for the victim." He waved a hand. "The motive would then be revenge."

"Ahh, I see. If the motive is revenge, then it could be a slight he did to someone and not even have known." Böðvarsson sighed. "That will make it even harder to discover the killer."

Hawke agreed in his head, but he didn't want the

detective to think he'd given up.

Someone rapped on the door and an officer stuck their head in. "We found something on the tapes."

Both men surged to their feet and followed the officer to the tech room.

The woman, who had helped Hawke before, sat in front of a monitor. "Here is your suspect waiting at the corner and getting into a cab."

It did appear to be the same coat and build. But they only had the back of the person.

"Are there any shots that get this person from the front?" Hawke asked. "Did the suspect come out of the Harpa?"

"Yes. They came out of the Harpa, but this camera only picked the person up at the door."

"What about from across the street?" Hawke asked.

"By the time we zoom in, the photo is too grainy to make out anything," the other officer said.

"Damn! Either this person is real lucky or this was well planned." Hawke paced back and forth. "He had to have slipped up somewhere."

"Keep going over the tapes. Try enlarging to see if you can find anything that might help us get an idea of who this is. And try to pick them up on cameras in the Harpa," Böðvarsson said. "Come on back to my office and go through the files."

Hawke followed the detective wondering if they would get a break in the case soon enough to capture the killer before they ended up back home.

Darkness had descended on Reykjavik when Hawke and Böðvarsson stepped out of the police station.

"I will take you to your hotel," the detective said.

Hawke didn't want to leave the police station. They had to discover who would have it out for Nonni. "Did you ever get Nonni's computer?"

"Yes, it is in the tech lab."

"Has anyone gone through it?" There had to be something somewhere to show he'd had an altercation with someone. It was evident they couldn't ask his friends since they'd kept vital information from the police.

"I haven't received a report, so I would say, no." Böðvarsson crossed his arms. "I can't allow you to stay here all night."

"Then I'll take the computer with me." Hawke grabbed the door handle of the police building.

The detective threw his hands in the air. "I will check it out to you, but it must be returned in the morning. I'm only doing this because our techs worked on the surveillance tapes all day." They both walked back in the building. Böðvarsson led him to the tech room, walked in, found the laptop still in an evidence bag and handed it to Hawke. "You will be here in the morning with this."

"I will have it here first thing." Hawke shoved the laptop into his backpack.

As the detective drove through Reykjavik he asked, "How will you get in? I'm sure there is a password."

"I'll figure it out." He had a thought. "Actually, drop me off at the Marina Hotel."

Böðvarsson glanced over at him. "Why there?"

"Ásta's comment about Riku and Nonni being in love. She would be more help to me than his so-called friends." He added. "Since Riku told us how the others seemed to be hiding things, I don't think she went out clubbing with them tonight."

"That is logical." Böðvarsson pulled up in front of the Marina Hotel. "Let me know if you discover anything."

"I will." Hawke slid out and walked into the lobby of the hotel. He texted Riku.

Are you in the hotel? May I come to your room? Need help with something.

A reply came right back. *I am here. Room 256. On my way.*

He shoved his phone in his pocket and headed for the elevator. A waving motion to his left caught his attention. He glanced over and moaned. Sigga and Largess.

"What are you doing here?" the woman asked.

"Tracking down leads." He stepped into the elevator and wished he'd walked out of the hotel, because Sigga stepped in, dragging Largess along with her.

"What leads?" She stood too close for Hawke's liking.

He took a step back and hit the wall of the elevator. "Mostly dead-end ones."

"It's got to be hard trying to find out who killed Nonni. He was a good guy," Largess said.

"You said you visit with the family when you're here. Tell me about them? Did they all get along?" Hawke flicked a gaze at Sigga. She frowned.

"They seemed like a happy family. I mean other than losing their older son to drugs. I think that put a strain on Einar and his wife, but they didn't quarrel or talk bitter to each other." Largess glanced down at

Sigga. "She knows Einar better than I do."

Hawke stopped his jaw from dropping open as the elevator dinged and the doors opened. He glanced at the floor and stepped out. To his relief, the doors closed and he remained standing in the hallway alone. He wondered if the man thought Sigga knew Einar better because they were both Icelanders or that he knew of her sleeping with the victim's father.

Following the signs, he found room 256 and knocked.

Mr. Tanaka answered the door, he motioned for Hawke to enter.

"Thank you for allowing your daughter to help me," Hawke said, pulling Nonni's laptop out of his backpack.

"We both would like to know who ended Nonni's life," Mr. Tanaka said. "I will get Riku." He walked to a door on one of the walls and knocked. The door opened and Riku walked through.

She had given him her father's room, not hers. "Mr. Hawke, I am willing to help you all I can."

"Good. We need to get into Nonni's computer." He started it up and waited for it to ask for a password. When that screen appeared, he tried her name. That didn't work. "Any idea what he would use for a password?"

"He wished to be a crime fiction novelist."

Hawke tried all different variations of the words. Nothing.

"Maybe it is numbers?" Mr. Tanaka said.

"Good idea." Hawke studied the screen. "What is your birthday?"

Riku recited the numbers. They didn't work.

"When did you meet Nonni? The date?"

Riku and her father discussed it in Japanese and she recited numbers.

The program opened.

A tear trickled down Riku's blushing cheeks. "He used when we met as a password," she said in a whisper.

The documents had three with titles that sounded like books. Hawke swallowed a lump in his throat. The young man would never finish these or see if he would be published. One document was titled 'Ideas'. Hawke assumed they were book ideas. He clicked on it anyway.

It appeared to be ideas on how to persuade the Westons to drop the suit against Nonni and the conference. They weren't illegal though a bit on the sketchy side. The one, meet Billy where we can't be seen and try to discuss what we can do to change our father's minds, set off bells. What if forensics was off on the time they believed Nonni was killed? Billy had a car and could have killed the budding writer at ten and drove back into town in time to pick up Ásta and have too much to drink with his lunch to make sure he was memorable.

Hawke typed this into a text message to Böðvarsson and sent it.

"Did you find something?" Riku asked.

"I'm not sure." Hawke clicked out of that document and opened the email.

The young woman sitting at the table beside him had sent many emails. There was also one from Billy, saying he'd meet with Nonni on Wednesday. Was that why Nonni had wanted to be the person they tracked?

He planned to meet Billy before everyone arrived? Another piece he mentioned to Böðvarsson in a text.

There was a folder in the email marked Wanza. Hawke clicked it and started reading the first email exchange.

"Did Nonni talk to you about Wanza?" He could tell by the emails Nonni was trying to help the other young woman. He talked of the college in Reykjavik and housing.

"Yes. He was helping her to get a visa and come study here." Riku smiled. It was evident she didn't feel the other young woman was a threat to her friendship with Nonni.

Hawke nodded. "It seems that she was going to do that and then three months later, she stopped replying to his emails." He wrote down Wanza's email address and sent another text to Böðvarsson. *Did you ever find Wanza or her mother?*

The emails didn't give any details into the young woman's life at all. Just she wanted to come to Iceland to continue her studies. He wondered about money. Hawke glanced at Riku. "Did Nonni say how Wanza planned to pay for college and a place to live?"

"Public college here is free. Just a small registration fee. She would have lived with Bragi." Riku glanced toward her father.

Hawke understood her hesitation. "Mr. Tanaka, could you order up coffee?"

The man nodded and walked to the phone on the other side of the room.

Riku leaned close. "She and Bragi became close. They were going to live together while she went to school and see if they wished to marry."

Hawke studied the young woman. She spoke the truth. "Why would Wanza stop emailing Nonni after three months? Do you think she found someone else back home?"

Riku shrugged. "She was young. Only seventeen."

"Seventeen? She shouldn't have been going to bars."

"If you were with Nonni and his friends, the people at the bars didn't pay attention to your age."

"And Bragi slept with her?" Hawke had figured that out from the first mention of Wanza.

"She told everyone, but me, she was twenty. I did not say anything. I did not think it would hurt. And being with all of us brought her out of the dark place she was in."

Hawke wondered if the girl had slipped back into the darkness after three months and that was why she'd stopped emailing or contacting anyone from here.

His phone buzzed. Böðvarsson.

A knock at the door meant his coffee was here. While the father and daughter gathered the tray, cups, tea and coffee pots from the bellboy, Hawke walked across the room to stand by the window and talk to the detective.

Chapter Nineteen

"We should have made the computer a priority," Böðvarsson said when Hawke answered the phone.

"Yeah. After seeing the note about meeting Billy at a remote setting, I wondered about the time of death. Any chance Forensics is off?"

"I'm sure they would be the first to say, with a body that falls in a boiling mud pool the time could be off. Do you think Billy is the one in the videos wearing the coat?"

"If he's been here for a week, he would have had time to check out the surveillance cameras. You'll need to have the techs go through the tapes from the time Billy arrived until Wednesday to see if he's seen in the Marina Hotel, my hotel, and looking around Harpa."

"Why did you bring up Wanza Odeyna?" Böðvarsson asked.

"Because she keeps coming up. Nonni's friends,

Riku Tanaka, and Nonni had all kept in contact with her until she stopped emailing three months after she went home. They say she was in a bad place when she came here, but became happy while here and was working with Nonni on coming here to go to school. Remember our theory is revenge?"

He had a feeling something happened to Wanza while she was in Iceland. And the only person she was emailing was Nonni, making him the target for revenge. But by who and why?

"I see what you are thinking. I will step up our hunt for Wanza and her mother. And we should have kilometers determined on the car Billy borrowed on Wednesday to determine if he drove to Krýsuvík which would mean that Kevin's rental may have been borrowed by someone other than the murderer. Good night."

Hawke didn't buy that. Why was the key stolen and returned so skillfully to avoid being seen? He had to agree with Billy borrowing from Ásta #2, it would have been quicker and easier for him to meet up with Nonni, kill him, and pick up Ásta #1 for his alibi. So why did his gut tell him the person who borrowed Largess's car was the killer? But his head was saying Billy was the killer?

"You are through with call?" Mr. Tanaka asked, standing at the table laid out with tea, coffee, and cookies.

"Yes." He smiled at the father and daughter and returned to his seat in front of the laptop. He closed the computer and picked up the cup of coffee. "Thanks."

"Did Nonni ever talk to you about Billy Weston?" Hawke asked.

Riku stared into her cup. "Only that he was angry Billy and his father were trying to make money off their incomp-incompay-"

"Incompetence."

"Yes, that is the word. He did not like that they could ruin his father and the conference."

"Did Nonni say what he planned to do about it?" Hawke sipped his coffee and watched the father and daughter exchange a glance.

Mr. Tanaka cleared his throat. "He planned to offer them money and pay the lawyer fees the Westons had acquired."

Hawke studied the man. "Do they have that kind of money? Nonni and Einar?"

"I do not know. I had offered to help out," Mr. Tanaka shrugged. "Nonni said it was not necessary."

"If Nonni and his father were willing to pay, there wasn't any reason for Billy to kill Nonni. Unless he wanted revenge more than the money." He was thinking out loud. It was something he did all the time because he was usually in the woods with his horses and dog or alone in his truck or his apartment.

"You think Nonni was killed for revenge?" Riku asked.

Hawke shook himself and studied the young woman. He should have kept his thought in his head. Worry wrinkled her brow and drew the corners of her lips down.

"I can't come up with any other reason. On the surface, there is no reason anyone would want to kill him. He was good to people, made them feel good, and cared about doing what was right." He stopped and held up a finger. "Except he was meeting in secret with Billy to talk over a money deal when he could have gone through the attorney…"

Hawke picked up his phone and texted Böðvarsson. *Find out who the lawyer was working for Westons on the defamation case.*

"You think the attorney learned of the meeting and planned to stop it so he could keep getting money?" Mr. Tanaka asked.

"It's as plausible as anything else we've come up with."

Riku yawned.

"It's late. I'll let you two get some sleep." He packed up the laptop and walked to the door.

"And you? Will you get sleep tonight?" Riku asked.

Hawke shook his head. "I won't sleep until we have Nonni's killer. There isn't enough time before you all head home."

"But if it is the lawyer…?"

"Then I won't care if it takes a bit longer. Right now, we don't know for sure." He didn't dare tell them about the rental car keys and the taxi driver's trip to take whoever borrowed it to pick it up.

He stepped out into the hall, shouldered his pack, and headed for the elevator. It was eleven. He could grab a drink in the bar and hope it helped him sleep a couple of hours or he could go back to his room and go over the file one more time.

In the lobby, he glanced toward the bar and restaurant and then stepped out into the dark drizzling night. They had to get this figured out by tomorrow night. Monday morning, the conference participants would be headed home.

Buzzing by his ear woke Hawke. He raised his head up off the open file on the table in his hotel room and stared at his cell phone. Dani.

"Hello?" he answered with a voice that sounded like he'd been battling a fire for three days.

"Wow! Rough night partying?" Dani asked, her voice full of humor.

"Not partying. Fell asleep rereading my notes on the homicide." He ran a hand through his hair and smacked his mouth, trying to add more moisture.

"You haven't figured it out? You don't have much time left."

"I know. That's why I was up most of the night trying to make sense of what we know already." He walked over to the sink and ran the water. When it was cold, he filled a cup and drank.

"Didn't mean to stir up a sore subject. Just checking in to make sure the weather conditions hadn't changed since we last talked. I want to make sure I have proper clothing while I'm there."

"It's still cold, windy, and a mixture of rain and sleet depending on where you are." Which reminded him of the person in the fur trimmed hooded coat. The person who had to be the killer. But who were they?

"I'll be busy today and maybe tomorrow when you get here. Can you take the bus from the airport? If you catch the right one, you'll be dropped off right in front of the Harpa where the conference being held. The hotel where we're staying is across the street."

"I'm a big girl. I know you'll be occupied with your homicide. Don't worry about me. I tagged myself onto your trip."

A smile relieved the tension in his face. That's one of the reasons he liked this woman. She understood duty. "I'll see you tomorrow."

"Can't wait." Dani ended the conversation and his phone buzzed.

Böðvarsson. Apparently, the detective hadn't slept much either.

"Hawke," he answered.

"Have you been up all night? You answered the phone quickly." Böðvarsson sounded more awake than Hawke felt.

"A good portion. A friend called." He didn't elaborate. No one needed to know he had a woman joining him.

"I discovered the lawyer. I called and have a breakfast meeting with him. Care to join me?"

"Yes, I would. What time?" Hawke glanced down at his wrinkled clothes from yesterday.

"I'll be by in thirty minutes to pick you up." Böðvarsson ended the call.

Hawke tossed his phone on the bed and walked into the bathroom. A quick shower and shave and he'd be ready to meet the lawyer.

Hawke shook hands with the man Böðvarsson introduced as the lawyer for the Westons. On the way to the restaurant, the detective had suggested Hawke take the lead on the questioning, since he knew more about what had been about to transpire than he did.

"You are American?" Egilsson asked.

"Yes. I'm with the Oregon State Police." Hawke set his badge on the table at the man's elbow.

"Why are you working with our police?" The

lawyer glanced at Böðvarsson.

"I found Jón Einarsson's body." He studied the short, round man as he seemed to be sizing up what had been said. "You did know that Einar Liefsson's son, Nonni, had been killed? It's been all over the news."

The man inhaled, "Yes, of course. I didn't realize that you were included in the investigation. There hasn't been any mention of you." Egilsson gave Böðvarsson a piercing glare.

Hawke had no idea why it would be a problem that he was helping with the investigation and it hadn't been broadcasted over the television.

"Did you know that Billy and Nonni were meeting to come to an agreement to settle the defamation suit?" Hawke wasn't going to give this man time to fancy talk his way out of anything.

"I know that Billy is here, in Reykjavik. He and I met when he first arrived. He brought more instructions from his father." He'd danced around the fact the two young men had been working outside of his supervision.

"So, you didn't know that Einar and Nonni were planning to settle outside of court?" Hawke persisted.

The man stared at him a glower pasted on his face.

"You did know. Was that what Billy was talking to you about?" Hawke pulled out Nonni's laptop and opened it up to the email between he and Billy setting up a meet on Wednesday. "This was the email where they set up the meeting to talk about settling outside of court."

Egilsson studied the email. "That's Nonni's computer."

"Yes. It was given to us by his parents to help us

find out who killed him." Hawke peered into the round face of the lawyer. "Did you know about this meeting? If so, what did you tell Billy?"

The lawyer picked up his coffee cup, sipped, and set it back down. Stalling. "I knew the young men were going to meet. I did not know what they were planning to discuss, other than Billy said Nonni was desperate to save his father and the conference. I gave him a figure that I felt could be raised that would cover my fees and be a good settlement for the Westons."

"Did Billy get back to you on what Nonni said?" Hawke wondered if Billy had killed Nonni then came back and told the lawyer that Nonni and his father refused to pay that much?

"He did tell me that we'd have to deal with the father. The son wasn't rational." Egilsson picked up his coffee cup.

"Was that Wednesday afternoon?" Böðvarsson asked this question.

The lawyer put his coffee cup down and nodded his head.

Böðvarsson stood, pulled his phone out of a pocket, and strode away from the table.

"Did you wonder if Billy had killed Nonni when you heard he was found dead Wednesday afternoon?" Hawke watched the man for any sign of discomfort.

"I, like many others, had been led to believe it was a random act of violence."

Hawke pressed his back against the chair and stared at the man. How he wished he could sweep a death under the rug so easily. He stood and followed Böðvarsson out of the restaurant. With what the lawyer said, it meant that Billy had met Nonni on Wednesday.

Now to pull him in to see if he'd spill about killing Nonni, and to find the proof he was at Krýsuvík during the time of death.

Chapter Twenty

Mid-morning Sunday, Hawke sat in the interview room with Böðvarsson, Billy Weston, and his lawyer, Egilsson. The young man had lawyered up as soon as he'd arrived at the station, even though they'd told him they just wanted to clarify his statement from the other day.

Billy grinned and Egilsson scowled. Neither one answering a single question Böðvarsson asked.

A knock on the door broke the awkward silence. An officer brought in a piece of paper, handing it to the detective.

Böðvarsson grinned. "We have added up the kilometers on the car you borrowed from the redheaded Ásta and it seems there are just enough kilometers unaccounted for to have taken you to Krýsuvík and back."

Hawke wanted to yell hallelujah. How would

Weston talk himself out of this?

"I don't understand? How can you figure out the kilometers? I borrowed a car." Weston stared at one then the other of them. "You made this up to make it look like I did it."

"No, we contacted the garage that maintains Ásta's car and received the miles it had on the odometer two weeks ago. Then we asked Ásta for an accounting of where she had driven since then and added the miles you said you drove and there is a difference that matches you meeting Nonni at Krýsuvík on Wednesday."

Weston shook his head.

Egilsson touched Weston's arm and leaned to whisper in his ear. They conversed a minute and the lawyer opened his hands.

"My client will tell you what he does know. He did drive out to Krýsuvík to meet Nonni, but he didn't see him. He did see the police cars and a bus leaving the parking lot where he was to meet Nonni at three."

Hawke stared at Weston. "I took down all the license plates of the vehicles in the parking lot right after the bus left."

Böðvarsson stood. "Remain here while we check to see if Ásta's license was one of them."

Out in the hall Bodvarrson turned to Hawke. "If you did write down that license, we can't hold him. He couldn't have been there at the time of the death and the car still there when he says he was there at three."

Hawke nodded. "Damn! I thought we had the killer."

They walked into Böðvarsson's office and checked the car plates. One of the numbers matched that of the red headed Ásta's car.

Hawke cursed and the detective picked up a folder on his desk. He handed the folder to Hawke.

Wanza Odeyna, daughter of Mari Odeyna, died in 2019. Her mother died of suicide a month later. Hawke stared at Böðvarsson. "Can you get more information on this? Riku and Nonni's friends said Wanza was in a bad place when she arrived. Can you find out if Wanza took her life, and if both she and her mother suffered from mental illness?"

"How can this have anything to do with our homicide?" Böðvarsson took the sheet of paper and slipped it into the growing one on Nonni's death.

"I don't know, but her name keeps coming up." Mari? Where had he heard that name before?

"I'll go let Billy loose."

The second the door closed, Hawke pulled out his notes and scanned the ones he'd taken from the people who were on the bus that day. Kanika said she sat next to Mari on her way out to Krýsuvík.

He dug through his papers to find the one with the list of people who took his class. There wasn't a Mari signed up for it.

How could she have sat next to Mari if there wasn't one? And what was her connection to the woman and her daughter?

When Böðvarsson returned, Hawke told him about his discovery. "Can you find out her connection to the Odeynas?"

"We can bring her in and question her." Böðvarsson said.

"We need some kind of proof to get a warrant to search her room. If we can find that coat in her possession, I'd feel a whole lot better about bringing her in." Hawke studied the forensic report. "Have they come up with anything else in forensics?"

"Halla sent me another report this morning. I haven't had time to look at it." Böðvarsson pulled a paper out of his file on the case. "They recovered fibers from a rock that also had Nonni's hair and blood on it. They are wool fibers from the sheep in our country."

"Which means either an Icelander or someone who purchased a pair of gloves killed him." Hawke stared at the papers in front of him. Anyone who came to the conference could have purchased a pair of gloves. "We have to find the coat in her possession."

"We cannot look for a coat without a warrant, and we cannot get a warrant without probable cause." Böðvarsson tossed the file on his desk. "It is Sunday. A day I don't work. I am going home, enjoying my family, and will decide what to do about the homicide tomorrow morning. I suggest you take the day to relax as well."

Hawke stood. He knew when he was being kicked out. But he wasn't going to relax. He was going to hang out at the last day of the conference and find a way to start up a conversation with Kanika. This was a long shot. All the other possibilities had been crossed off his suspect list.

He called a taxi and asked to be dropped off at the Harpa. It was Sunday afternoon. Only a few classes were still going. Hawke climbed the stairs and went straight to the base of operations room. Einar wasn't present but the tech woman, Dóra, sat in front of the computer.

"Hello. Have you gone to any of the classes you

signed up for?" she asked.

"No. I've been busy. Can you tell me if Kanika," he pulled out the list from the people who attended his class and read, "Tumaini, is still here? I remember we marked how long we were staying after the conference. And could you tell me if she is going on the Snow Jeep tour tomorrow?"

The woman studied him before she started tapping on the keyboard. "You have come in and asked about several people. Are they all suspects in Nonni's death?"

He didn't say anything. The less she or anyone else knew, the better.

"Here she is. Kanika is leaving on a plane tomorrow afternoon. She is signed up for the three o'clock class in the Ríma Room." She pointed down. "On the first floor."

"Thank you." He started to leave and had a thought. "Any chance you know if she's rooming with anyone and who it might be?"

Dóra typed some more and wrote on a piece of paper. "This is who we have down but that doesn't mean things haven't changed since they registered."

"Thank you." Hawke plucked the paper from her and stared at the name. Rowena Albright. There wasn't a room number, but he knew it was the second floor and could ask at the desk for Rowena and not make Kanika suspicious.

Hawke walked down to the first floor and found a place to wait for the class to get over. He put Rowena's name into the search app on his phone. There were several. He picked the first one from England. She was Caucasian. Carmilla had called her a black woman when he'd asked about the women in Largess's room on Tuesday night. He clicked out of that one and clicked the next one in England. It was a black woman. She had a nice smile. Her husband was Caucasian. He was a doctor with an English title. Hawke wondered how he felt about his wife working in… He read some more. She wasn't in law enforcement. She was in the medical field and worked with the British SAR. She was from Machakos, Kenya. Her husband had been working with Doctors Across Borders when they met.

Hawke stopped reading. What had Bragi said? Wanza was from something Macha. He continued reading. Rowena's maiden name was Mwinga.

He flipped through the papers in his folder. He didn't have the information about Wanza and her mother. Pulling out his phone, Hawke texted Böðvarsson. *What are Mari Odeyna and Kanika Tumaini's maiden names?*

People started filing out of the Ríma room. Hawke shoved his papers and file back into his pack and stood. There had been a photo of Rowena from several years earlier on the information he'd brought up on his phone. He saw her before he noticed Kanika walking beside her. Kanika wore a polo shirt, khaki slacks, and running shoes. Rowena had dress slacks, a button-up shirt, and shoes his mom called Mary Janes. He'd never been able to figure out why. They were a fancy looking shoe with a flat heel and strap across the top of the foot.

He fell into step behind them. They were talking in a language he figured had to be Kenyan. It wasn't Icelandic or English. When the main group headed for the stairs or elevator, the two he was interested in headed for the outside doors.

Once they were all three outside, Hawke spoke.

"Evening."

They both flinched, but turned in unison and smiled.

"Hawke. Where have you been? We have barely seen you since Wednesday," Kanika said.

"I've been trying to find Nonni's killer." He studied them both. Neither one seemed upset with what he blurted out. "Who is your friend?"

"Oh, you haven't met Rowena?" Kanika flicked a hand toward the other woman. "This is my roommate for the conference. Rowena Albright from London."

Hawke held out a hand.

The woman shook hands and smiled. "And you, Mr. Hawke, where are you from?"

"Oregon, in the United States. And it's just Hawke." He motioned the direction of the Marina Hotel. "Shall we continue to the hotel?"

They glanced at one another, pulled their coats closer around their necks and started walking.

"What class did you find the most useful at the conference?" he asked by way of starting up a conversation they were less likely to run away from.

"Because I'm more on the medical side of SAR, I enjoyed the one about what medical supplies each member should carry and how to keep the supplies up to date," Rowena said.

"And you?" Hawke asked.

Kanika glanced at him then ahead as they continued walking. "I would have said your class if it hadn't ended the way it did. I would have to say the base of operations workshop was what I needed to learn more about."

As she talked, Hawke heard inflections that might

be mistaken as British. His heart hammered in his chest. Had he discovered Nonni's killer finally? Rowena had a distinctive British accent. Either woman had a husky voice that could sound male if they tried.

All of this was just circumstantial. He had to find proof.

"Are you going on the Super Jeep tour tomorrow?" he asked.

Kanika nodded. "Rowena talked me into staying to go. I will never get to Iceland again. I want to see as much of it as I can."

"Are you staying the rest of the week?" Hawke asked, feeling as if a weight had been lifted if she would be around longer.

"No, I leave first thing Tuesday morning. I cannot afford to be away from work any longer than that."

That only gave him one more day to discover if she killed Nonni. "Since you suggested Kanika attend the Super Jeep tour, I take it you are going?" he asked Rowena.

"Yes. Like Kanika, this may be the only time I'm here and I want to see as much of it as I can. My husband is flying in Tuesday, and we're going to vacation for a week." She shook her head. "But he usually wants to see things that are inside. I like seeing nature. Are you going on the tour?"

"I haven't decided. I have a friend flying in tomorrow."

At the hotel the women went straight to the elevator.

It would be awkward if he followed them into the elevator and to their door. And they didn't seem interested in inviting him up to continue the conversation. He stopped at the registration desk and waved. "Have safe trips home."

When the elevator doors closed, Hawke took up a seat in the lobby where he could see who came out of the elevators before they saw him.

Chapter Twenty-one

"What are you doing here?" Sigga's voice jolted Hawke from the space in his head where he was tracking all the information on the case.

He glanced up and found her standing three feet from him. He'd been so intent on his thoughts and staring at the elevator that he'd allowed her to sneak up on him.

"Waiting." His phone buzzed. Böðvarsson. He motioned for the woman to sit in the chair beside his while he answered the phone.

"Hawke."

"I told you to relax for the rest of the day," the detective said.

"I can't. What can you tell me?"

"You do know who Rowena Albright's husband is, don't you?" He'd not heard apprehension in Böðvarsson's voice before.

"No. Who is Mr., or should I say, Dr. Albright?"

Sigga snorted and shook her head.

Hawke frowned. "Who is he then?"

"Only one of the top Doctors in England and a relative to the royals."

"I didn't ask for his background or his wife's. I asked about Mari Odeyna and Kanika Tumaini." Hawke had never played favorites with anyone.

"Mari Odeyna was cousins with Rowena Albright. As for Kanika, so far we haven't pulled up any connection between her and Mari."

Hawke stared at the elevators. It would be even harder to get the information if their killer was Rowena.

"Good thing we didn't drag Kanika in here, now isn't it?" Böðvarsson said.

Tugging the stocking cap from his head, Hawke gave his scalp a good scratch while he thought. "They're both going on the Super Jeep tour to the glacier tomorrow. I've just decided to go." He ended the conversation and turned his attention to Sigga, who had been listening to every word.

"Why did you want to know about a Mari Odeyna and Kanika? And what did it have to do with the Albrights?" Sigga leaned closer. "You don't think they had anything to do with Nonni, do you?"

Hawke stood. While he was ninety percent sure Sigga had nothing to do with Nonni's death, he shouldn't tell her what he suspected.

But she was on the same hallway as the two women he wanted to keep eyes on. "Invite me up to your room."

She smiled. "Is this a business or pleasure invite?"

"Business."

Her smile remained bright. "Does this mean you believe I didn't kill Nonni?"

He just smiled and led her to the elevators.

They didn't say anything until they were in her room.

"Do you know which room is Rowena and Kanika's?" Hawke asked.

"Three down on the left. Are you going to use my room for surveillance?" Sigga opened a bottle of water. "I have a date tonight with Kevin. I don't care if you stay here while I'm gone, but if you need my help, I can cancel."

"I need to get into their room."

Sigga stared at him. "They didn't use a weapon that you can find."

"I'm not looking for a weapon. I'm looking for clothing. The ones we saw the person wearing when they hailed a cab, left the message about you and men and the keys to Largess's rental car." Hawke paced to the window and back again. "Even if I find the clothes, we have to come up with something to get a warrant to legally find the clothing."

His mind latched onto something else. "Why is Mrs. Albright rooming with someone? Wouldn't someone with her money and status stay in a suite or something?"

"If I was married to Dr. Albright, I'd be staying in the hotel suite, that's for sure. In fact, I wouldn't even be here." Sigga sat on the bed, crossing her legs and sipping the bottle of water.

"Exactly. Why is she here, unless it is for revenge?"

"I don't understand? What are you talking about

184

revenge?"

Hawke relayed what they had discovered about Wanza and Mari Odeyna.

"That's horrible! You think, what? That Wanza hit another downward spiral of depression, killed herself, and then her mother couldn't take it and killed herself?" Sigga stared at him with disbelief on her face.

"It's the only thing I can think of. Nonni had no enemies other than Billy Weston and his father. Billy is here, but he has alibis for the time of death. He was planning to meet Nonni to talk about a settlement, but Nonni was killed before they met." Hawke walked to the door and peeked out. There was movement down the hall in the direction Sigga had said the women were staying.

They passed by the door. One of them was wearing the fur-lined hooded parka. It was Rowena Albright.

He closed the door. "Follow them and see where they go?"

Sigga picked up her coat and purse and hurried out the door. "I'll cancel Kevin."

Hawke waited until he was sure the three women were on the ground floor and he took the elevator to the lobby. He texted Böðvarsson. *Rowena Albright is wearing a coat that matches the one in the surveillance tapes.*

Before he set foot out the door, his phone rang.

"I told you not to bother Rowena." A hint of worry fluttered the detective's words.

"I'm only interested in discovering the truth. Sigga is following them. When I know where they are, I'll mosey there and start up a conversation and see if she clams up."

"I don't want to deal with my commissioner because you said something offensive to Rowena."

"I won't. I'll only bring up Wanza." Hawke's phone made a noise.

Sigga texted. *They are at Fish Company restaurant.* She added a marker on a map for him to follow.

Thanks.

"Hawke? Hawke?" Böðvarsson drew him back to the conversation.

"I'm here. Sigga says they are at Fish Company. I'll join her and maybe we can start up a conversation." He disconnected and headed out the door, following the navigation app on his phone. The place appeared old, but nicely kept up. The main entrance was under a bridge. He discovered Sigga sitting inside the door.

"I cancelled Kevin and asked for a table close to Rowena and Kanika." She stood, spoke Icelandic to the hostess, and they were seated at a table next to the women he was interested in.

Kanika glanced up as they were being seated. She frowned and said something in Kenyan to Rowena. The other woman glanced their direction, smiled, and said something back.

"I hope they think we're here on a date." Sigga leaned across the table toward him. "Maybe you should order a bottle of wine to make it look like we aren't working."

Hawke didn't want to have a date with the Icelandic Chief Inspector, but he could tell Kanika was already suspicious of him showing up here and sitting next to them.

He waved the waiter over and suggested Sigga pick

a wine. After the wine was served and they approved, well, Sigga approved of it, Hawke picked up the menu. Luckily it was written in English. He glanced over at Sigga's and noted it was written in Icelandic.

Hawke ordered a main course of fish and settled back, trying to look at ease when he wished he could understand what the two at the other table were talking about.

Sigga sipped the wine and asked, "Have you and Böðvarsson discovered any reason someone would want to kill Einar's son?"

He started to glare at her, but noticed the women at the table next to them had stopped conversing.

"We're running out of suspects. The two we thought were possibilities, have airtight alibis." He picked up his wine and sipped. It wasn't bad. Not as bitter as he remembered wine being. Though he would have preferred a beer, having wine would keep him from drinking too much.

"Where does that leave you?" Sigga leaned back as her food arrived. The plate was piled with food.

Hawke had been afraid with the atmosphere, which was elegant as well as cozy, that the food would be skimpy while the price was high. His plate was placed in front of him and he was glad the two next to them had picked this restaurant for dinner.

"We believe it has to be connected to the conference, why else would the killer have struck now." He was pleased to see the fish was done but not dry. Just the way he liked it. The bite made him groan with delight. The flavor of fish and the sauce on it, were a perfect pairing.

Sigga smiled at him. "I told you the food here was

excellent."

He grinned. The policewoman was good at surveillance. Quick to say things that sounded natural. "You were right. I'm glad you dragged me here."

"If you believe the homicide is connected to the conference, shouldn't you look at people angry with Einar?" Sigga picked up her wine glass.

"We are. Again, those haven't panned out any better than the ones who had a problem with Nonni." He ate a couple more bites, listening to see if the two women had started chatting. Their food was about finished. They shoved their plates to the side. Their bottle of wine was still half full. Hopefully, they would stick around and finish it off. Hawke didn't want to walk away from this tasty food.

"But you talked to Nonni's friends. What did they have to say?" Sigga asked, slipping a bite of her lamb dish into her mouth.

"They can't think of anything, though we did find he'd corresponded with a Wanza Odeyna for several months after she was here with her mother two years ago." An intake of breath from the other table let him know they were listening. He took a bite.

"Were they lovers?" Sigga asked.

"I don't think so. They were discussing Wanza coming here to go to college. He sent her applications for the school and a visa." He waited, but no one from the other table jumped in. Hawke cast a glance that direction. Rowena was listening intently. Kanika was sipping wine.

"What happened?" Sigga asked, now leaning in, as if the story was the most fascinating thing she'd ever heard.

"We discovered Wanza died and then a month later so did her mother." Hawke shrugged. "We are uncertain if they both contracted a disease or if something else killed them."

"What would that have to do with Nonni?" Sigga asked, sitting back in her chair.

"Nothing that we know of, but it's the only other thing we can find that is unusual with Nonni's life." He sighed. "Wish we knew more about their deaths. Böðvarsson is working on that."

The two next to them said something and stood as if to leave.

"That's a gorgeous coat," Sigga said to Rowena. "Did you get it here?"

Rowena smiled. "No, I brought it with me from home. Have a good night." She walked to the entrance of the restaurant without looking back. Kanika hurried to catch up.

"That didn't get anything out of them." Sigga clanked her fork down on the table.

Hawke grinned. "We learned that is Rowena's coat, and they left when we talked about Wanza. You don't always have to get the results you want to learn something new." He dug into his food. "Eat up. I'm tired of waiting for someone to get back to us from Kenya. Let's see if Dóra at the base of operations can use her computer skills to look up the obituaries on the mother and daughter."

Sigga stared at him. "You think she can do that?"

"We won't know until we ask."

"It's late, she might not even be there." Sigga scooped the rest of her meal into her mouth as Hawke called Einar.

Chapter Twenty-two

Hawke and Sigga sat in the base of operations room for the conference at the Harpa while Dóra tapped on the keyboard and asked questions.

Using the information about Mari Odeyna from the conference two years earlier, they had enough to know where she lived and where she'd worked.

Dóra pulled up the newspapers in the area for three to five months after the conference.

"The deaths have to be the reason for the revenge on Nonni. Do you think her mother didn't want Wanza to go to school in Iceland and that sent the girl into depression and she killed herself?" Sigga had been coming up with all kinds of reasons.

"We won't know until we have the truth." Hawke stood and walked over to the computer. "What are you finding?"

"Just the obit for the mother. Nothing on the girl. But it seems the mother took her life because of her sorrow over her daughter's death." She clicked more keys. "There weren't any accidents involving the daughter. But it's odd I can't find anything about her death other than the mother's obit."

"If the daughter had mental issues, do you think the mother did and she killed the daughter?" Sigga said what Hawke was starting to wonder about.

"But why would anyone take revenge for that?" Hawke paced the floor. "There has to be another reason."

"I'm digging into the information on the police station where the mother worked." She typed some more. "*Magnað*! They have a counselor for the department." She wrote on a piece of paper. "Here is the name and phone number."

Hawke took the paper and patted the woman's shoulder. "You are missing your calling working for the conference."

She grinned. "When I'm not doing this, I work in the cybercrimes department."

Hawke laughed and pulled out his phone. "What's the time difference between here and Kenya?"

"They're three hours ahead of us," Dóra said.

He glanced at his watch. Midnight in Kenya. "Damn! I'll have to wait and call in the morning."

"Not much more you can do tonight. Let's go." Sigga stood and put her coat on.

"Yeah, not much I can do." He walked to the door and stopped. "Thanks for this."

"Anything to find Nonni's killer." The woman stood. "Time for me to go home. There will be a lot to do in the morning, clearing out all the conference stuff."

Hawke held the door for her, and they walked down the stairs together. "How's Einar holding up?"

She shook her head. "I don't know what he'll do after we clean up. He won't have anything to focus on."

"Does he still work?"

"No. He retired and only does SAR work now."

"Then it will be tough." Hawke felt for the man. It would be hard to lose two children. It was a good thing he didn't have any. Though his mom didn't feel that way.

At the sidewalk in front of the Harpa, Dóra hailed a taxi, Sigga walked down the sidewalk toward the Marina Hotel, and Hawke crossed the streets to his hotel.

They'd lost momentum today, discovering they were looking at the wrong person. He had a feeling his call in the morning to the counselor in Kenya would clear up a lot.

Buzzing by his ear startled Hawke awake. He slapped at the annoying insect and his fingers touched the screen on his phone.

"Hawke? Hawke? I landed. I'll get a car and be there as soon as I can." Dani's voice had his hands gripping the phone.

"Good. I thought you were taking the bus?" he said, sitting up. At least he hadn't slept in his clothes this time.

"I decided we'd need a car to travel around."

"That makes sense. I won't be here, when you arrive, but I'll let the hotel know you're coming," He glanced down at the opposite side of the bed.

"Thank you. See you when I see you." The call

ended.

The folder, all the papers, and photos were scattered across the bed. He'd been reading through them one more time when he must have fallen asleep.

It was seven in the morning. He had an hour to get to the Marina Hotel and catch the Super Jeep tour.

Hawke dressed quickly, grabbing all the warm clothing he'd brought with him. Pulling the stocking cap onto his head, he headed to the elevator. In the lobby, he let the clerk know that Dani Singer would be arriving and to give her a key to his room.

Out on the sidewalk walking toward the Marina Hotel, he dialed the number Dóra had given him for the police psychiatrist in Nairobi.

The woman who answered said something in a language Hawke thought sounded like what the two women in the table next to them last night had been using.

"Hello, I'm Gabriel Hawke, with the police in the United States. I'd like to speak with Dr. Mutambe, please."

"Hello. He is with a patient right now. May I have your number for him to return call?" The woman had a bit of a British accent but it was heavily accented with her nationality.

"Please. It's urgent I speak with him today." He didn't want to be put on a list and wait a week.

"What is this about?"

"A deceased patient."

"Dr. Mutambe is not that kind of doctor." Her tone was apologetic.

"I know what he does. It is one of his patients who has died. Mari Odeyna."

The woman drew in her breath. "I will give him the message."

He found the woman's reaction interesting. What about Mari's death would have her shrink's receptionist act surprised?

At the Marina Hotel, people already stood on the sidewalk, waiting for the bus to pick them up. They would go by bus to Húsafell and there get in the Super Jeeps for the tour of the glacier.

Hawke was surprised to see Böðvarsson sitting in his car in front of the hotel. The detective held up two cups of coffee and a bag that looked suspiciously like baked goods.

Hawke slid into the car, grasping the cup of coffee offered to him. "What are you doing here?"

"I wanted to know what you said to Rowena Albright last night before I arrive at the office and am told I have a call from the commissioner."

Hawke laughed. "I didn't say anything." He went on to retell how the night played out. "When Sigga admired the coat Rowena was wearing, which I'd stake my career is the same one in the surveillance tapes, she said she'd brought it from home."

Böðvarsson set down his coffee cup and pressed a fist to his sternum. "I was afraid of this when I learned she was related to the woman you are fixated on."

Hawke went on to tell him about the call he was waiting on.

"You asked Dóra to do police work when she was on vacation?" Böðvarsson acted as if that was a greater sin than blaming the wife of a prominent British doctor of murder.

"At the time, I didn't know she worked for the

police. I just thought she was a talented computer nerd."

His phone buzzed. Dr. Mutambe.

"Hello, this is Hawke."

"Gabriel Hawke? The policeman who wishes to know something about one of my former patients?" The man said it as if he were condemning him for even asking about Mari.

"Yes."

"I do not feel right talking to someone I do not know about this."

"I'm working with the Iceland Police to discover who killed a man. I think Mari and Wanza's deaths have something to do with it." Silence followed. He was just getting ready to say more when the doctor spoke.

"Who was killed in Iceland?"

Hawke took this to mean he knew the name already. "Jón Einarsson. Also called, Nonni."

The man mumbled something in the language Hawke didn't know.

"You know who the dead man is. It's because of Mari and Wanza, correct? And you might know who killed the young man?" Hawke wasn't going to let him think too long on how to save whoever did the killing.

"I do not know who could have killed him. But he is the person Mari accused of killing her daughter—Nonni and herself."

Hawke felt like he'd run out of oxygen and was losing track of the conversation. "Why would she accuse Nonni and herself of Wanza's death?"

"Wanza returned from Iceland much happier than I had seen her in years. She was doing well until Mari discovered why Wanza really wanted to go back to Iceland. She was pregnant. Her mother believed it was the man, Nonni, who was helping Wanza plan to leave Kenya and Mari." The doctor murmured something away from the phone and continued. "Mari had been a young mother without a husband. She'd struggled for years and did not want her daughter to do the same. For this reason, she forced Wanza to have an abortion. Only she caught infection from the procedure and died. A month after Wanza died, Mari took her own life. She couldn't live with the fact she'd caused her daughter's death." He sighed. "I told her to let the child go to Iceland. If nothing else the baby would come, and she would either marry and stay, living a good life, or she would come home. I learned of her forcing the child to the doctor after everything went wrong."

Hawke took it all in. Because Nonni had been the good person that he was, he had tried to help Wanza get back to Iceland. He wondered if the young man knew his friend had fathered a baby? If so, it didn't seem as if he'd told Bragi, the father. The person who, by accounts of the murderer, should have been the one who died.

"Thank you for all of this Dr. Mutambe. We had no idea who the killer could have been as the young man who died was not the father of Wanza's child. He was merely a friend helping a friend."

"Then the murder, as with all murders, was done for all the wrong reasons."

Hawke had to agree. "Yes." He ended the connection and turned to Böðvarsson. "The murderer killed the wrong person."

The detective stared at him.

Hawke repeated what the doctor had told him ending with, "Bragi is the one who slept with Wanza, not Nonni. He was killed because he is who they knew stayed in contact with her after she returned home."

"This doesn't go to anyone besides us," Böðvarsson said. "We don't need another death."

"Do we pressure Rowena about the coat and what we know about her cousin?" Hawke thought it might work with the cousin unless she lawyered up right away. But he had an inkling because of her comment about riding with Mari, that Kanika may have more to do with the murder than her roommate.

"Can you call Kanika's superior and find out how or if she knew Mari Odeyna?" Hawke grabbed a pastry from the bag as a bus rolled up. "I'll see what the two do on this excursion. There has to be a reason they are going." He studied the group. The two women were standing in line. Neither one wore the fluffy warm coat. He wondered why when it was going to be colder on the glacier than it had been walking around Reykjavik.

Chapter Twenty-three

Hawke climbed on board the bus and sat in a seat a couple rows behind the two women. He was pleased to see that only about twenty people were going on the trip. It would make keeping track of the two easier.

He'd nodded to both of the women as he'd walked by on his way to his seat. Rowena had smiled and nodded. Kanika just stared forward. They were an interesting duo. Knowing what he did about the two of them, he wondered if they were working together or Kanika was orchestrating the whole thing, using Rowena's grief.

Two hours on the bus, and they unloaded in a parking lot in Húsafell. Six Super Jeeps with drivers waited for them. The Jeeps were slightly larger than a regular four door Jeep and they had large tires. Not as outlandish as a Monster truck but twice as large as a normal pickup.

Hawke didn't want to be so obvious that he was tailing the two, therefore, he made certain he climbed into the Jeep behind the one the two women were in. He was pleased to see they were in the same Jeep as Leonard Harlow.

Harlow would try to carry on a conversation and would be sure to tell everyone he could if the two snubbed him.

When the Jeeps pulled onto the glacier covered with new snow, the drivers got out and released air out of the tires. When their driver climbed back in, he said, "Letting air out, gives better traction on the ice and snow."

They moved across the glacier as if they were floating, until a tire hit a rut. Then the steering wheel was jerked out of the driver's grip and the vehicle rocked back and forth. Hawke held onto the hand hold to keep his body from flopping onto the driver. The two people riding in the back "oophed and squeaked" as they rocked through the bumps. This happened half a dozen times before what appeared to be a large culvert with a tarp over the end appeared in the middle of nowhere. The Jeeps all stopped and people crawled out. Voices rejoiced at being out of the Jeeps and no longer bumping around. They were lucky to have a sunbreak. The white of the snow was blinding.

The trip across the glacier had taken an hour. The Jeep drivers explained to the group that one person would be the spokesperson for the tour. The rest of the drivers would remain on top and wait for them. Because there were less than twenty, everyone would enter at the same time. Hawke was glad he didn't have to noticeably try to get into a group with the two women.

He, instead, fell in step with Harlow.

"What did you think of the Jeep ride?" he asked the young man.

"Wow, there were a couple of times the two in the back seat shrieked when we rocked back and forth." The young man had a grin from ear to ear. "It was the coolest thing I've ever done."

Hawke laughed. He was pretty sure the two women wished they hadn't come. Which led him to wonder why they had. Even though Kanika was a policewoman, she didn't strike him as the outdoor type.

They walked down a slight incline on a mat that kept them from sliding or falling. At the bottom the SAR Jeep driver, and now guide for the tunnel, asked them to all put on crampons. The stretchy contraptions attached to the bottom of their shoes adding spikes to grip the icy floor.

"This will keep you from slipping as you walk through the tunnel," the guide said, while also running through the rules of the cave. As everyone straightened from putting on the spiked crampons, the guide walked deeper into the tunnel, talking about how it was manmade and one of the only ones that is open year-round for tourists.

The tunnel was around twelve to fifteen feet high with an arched ceiling and ten to twenty feet across in places. The ice on the sides was slick, grooved from the machinery used to cut it, and beautiful. It reminded him of coiled pottery. Hawke made a note to bring Dani here later in the week. He'd never been one to care for enclosed places but the size of the tunnel and the unique blue to the glacier ice made him forget he was 30 yards under the ice.

The group moved along the tunnel at a slow pace, giving Hawke a chance to locate Rowena and Kanika. They were hanging toward the back of the group.

"You cannot get lost. The tunnel makes a circle and comes out back at the main tunnel. There are two rooms designed for events such as weddings and parties. Once a year there is a secret solstice party held in the tunnel. DJs from around the world come and play music while people dance." The guide's voice carried well in the icy corridor. He stopped and allowed people to take photos of what appeared to be a small chapel with ice pews and altar. Hawke hung back by the entrance to the room. He didn't need any photos.

Even though they were enclosed in ice, it felt warmer than the air outside. Without wind and an even temperature, he pulled the stocking cap off his head. The knitted cap made him too hot.

Rowena and Kanika, again, hung back from the rest of the group. Their heads were together as if plotting something. Their behavior made him even more wary. Why had they come to the tunnel?

The group moved on to another room, took photos, and continued deeper into the ice tunnel. The lights strung along the tunnel, sparkled like large crystals of snow in the reflections on the smooth ice walls.

They came to a dugout area large enough for them to all stand in the middle of the blue light. This area was the heart of the glacier. The blue glow in the room was beautiful. Hawke felt as if he were in the center of the glacier experiencing what it would be like to be encased in the massive frozen ice. He wondered if this would be a similar feeling to being held in the bosom of Mother Earth.

Someone bumped him, drawing his thoughts back to the ice tunnel. He glanced around. Rowena and Kanika were missing. There were three tunnel entrances. The one they'd walked through, the one continuing, and a third. The guide said they had ten minutes to enjoy this room and wander the two small circles.

Hawke moved to the smaller tunnel that would have been the closest to the two women where he'd last seen them. He walked around a curve and tripped. His hands and arms kept his chin from connecting with the hard ice floor. Air whooshed out of his chest and his knees ached from cracking on the ice. The scratching sound of someone running in the crampons and a rushed whisper pushed him to his feet.

One of the women must have tripped him. Why? He bent his right leg. His knee burned and ached. That knee must have taken most of his weight when he went down.

"Hawke what are you doing?" Harlow's voice echoed down the corridor behind him.

"Stay here. I'll be right back." Hawke didn't look back, he continued as fast as his aching knees would carry him. He caught a glimpse of the two women back in the room the group had stopped in. He studied them. They were both focusing their cameras on different walls of the blue room. Studying them from head to toe, he realized the daypack Kanika wore looked as if it had deflated. They'd left something in the tunnel.

He backtracked to where Harlow stood. "Why did you tell me to stay here?"

"You can go now." Hawke waved the man to continue on down the side tunnel.

Three more of the conference attendees walked by, talking.

Hawke waited for them to pass by before he slowly walked along the tunnel. There was a spot, just a little wider than the rest of the tunnel where a large crack in the ice was visible. He walked over to the crack and peered down. The coat he'd been staring at on videos had been shoved into the crack where someone walking by and looking wouldn't see it.

Hoping the crack wouldn't open farther and pull him in, Hawke prayed to the Creator to not anger the glacier as he leaned in with one arm. His fingers barely touched the cloth.

He took off his daypack and pulled out a small roll of parachute cord.

"Everyone, we need to continue on," the guide's voice carried down the tunnel.

Hawke ignored the man's request. The coat in the crevice was evidence, that was the only reason the two women came on this trip. They wanted it gone. Had Sigga asking about the coat last night given them the idea to get rid of it today? But why here? They could have tossed it into the harbor? Whatever the reason they chose to put it here, he wasn't going to leave it in the crack.

A loop in the cording wasn't going to catch the coat. He dug in his pack for something that would hook the garment and pull it up just enough he could get a hold of it. He carried his file of Nonni's case. In it was a paperclip holding some papers together. He opened the clip, shoved one end through an end of the cording, making sure it was attached well, and made a hook out of the other end.

He leaned over the crack, navigating the paperclip down near the hood. The first attempt was a bust. The clip didn't hook. He bent it a bit wider and hooked the hood. Tugging on the cording, the hood came up enough he could reach in with his arm and pull the coat out.

The coat was rolled up and stashed in his daypack when Harlow came around a corner.

"Hawke what are you doing? The guide sent me in to find you the last place I'd seen you." His gaze landed on the cording on the floor of the tunnel.

Hawke grabbed the cord, rolled it up, and shoved it in the side pocket of his pack. "Are they waiting for me?" He strode along the tunnel with Harlow scratching behind him.

"Yes. They held one Jeep back for us." Harlow walked beside him. "What were you doing?"

"Nothing that needs repeated." Hawke stared at the young man.

"You weren't trying to do harm to the tunnel were you?" Harlow stopped, grabbing Hawke's coat sleeve.

"No." Hawke didn't want to tell him what he was doing. What he knew of Harlow, the man didn't seem capable of not telling everything he knew to anyone. "I dropped my camera while taking a photo. I tried to fish it out, but couldn't get it."

The man studied him a moment, muttered something, and hurried ahead of him.

At the spot where they'd put the crampons on, a new guide stood with another group of people. Hawke quickly took his ice spikes off and hurried up the culvert to the opening. It was growing dark and starting to snow. He understood why the guide wanted to get going.

Harlow took the front seat and left Hawke to sit with an attendee he'd not met.

The man stared at him. "What took you so long?"

"I had to make a stop at the outhouse," he said.

Harlow coughed. "It's called a WC here."

Hawke remembered seeing the sign for an emergency WC as they'd entered the tunnel and put on their crampons. "Right."

Harlow hadn't bought his story of losing his camera. He'd probably be even more interested in what he did since Hawke had changed his story for the man sitting next to him. He didn't care. He had the coat and he'd turn it over to Böðvarsson as soon as he saw the detective.

On the ride back to Reykjavik on the bus, Hawke texted with Böðvarsson. He didn't want anyone around him to hear the conversation. He'd sat in the front of the bus, ignoring the two women who'd tried to hide the coat.

Rowena and Kanika tried to ditch the coat. He texted.

Where?

The ice tunnel. I found it. It's in my pack.

Where are you now?

Hawke tapped the driver on the shoulder. "How much farther to the hotel?"

"Thirty minutes."

"Thanks."

30 out.

I'll pick you up.

Copy.

Hawke's phone buzzed. Dani.

"Hello," he answered. There wasn't anything in their conversation no one could overhear.

"Where are you?" Dani asked.

"Almost back to town. I went on that Super Jeep tour to the ice tunnel. We are going there later this week."

She laughed. "It's on my list. But if you've seen it already…"

"I want to see it with you." He hadn't meant for that to sound as intimate as it did.

"Oh, then we'll have to make sure we go. Will you be back to have dinner with me?"

"No. Detective Böðvarsson is picking me up. He wanted to tell me something he learned today." He would have enjoyed a meal with Dani and spending a couple hours not thinking about the murder.

"I'll see you when you get here, then." She ended the conversation before he had time to say he appreciated her acceptance of his job.

Chapter Twenty-four

Böðvarsson's car sat in the valet parking at the Marina Hotel when the bus pulled up to the door of the building.

Hawke was the first one off the bus. He hurried over to the car as fast as he could with a knee that ached. He tossed his pack in the back seat and dropped into the passenger seat.

"What happened to you? You didn't limp before?" Böðvarsson asked.

"One of the women tripped me while the other one stuffed the coat in a crevice. I've hurt worse." Hawke wasn't going to let a spill keep him from getting the two women arrested.

"Want something to eat?" the detective asked.

"Yes. I'm starving. But not here."

The man nodded and pulled out of the valet parking and onto the street. "I know a place on the wharf that has good food and a quiet atmosphere."

When they were settled at the restaurant on the second floor of an old building on the wharf and had ordered their meal, Detective Inspector Böðvarsson pulled his notepad out of his suit pocket.

"I had a long discussion with Kanika's superior. He didn't know where she was. She asked to take these two weeks off for vacation in February. He thought she was visiting relatives. She had to have used her own money to attend the conference and fly here."

"Around the one-year anniversary of Mari's death, she booked this conference." Hawke had a suspicion he knew what Böðvarsson was going to say next.

"Mari Odeyna and Kanika were partners on the police force in Machakos. When Mari took her life, he said, Kanika was put on leave for a month and sent to the psychiatrist."

"It sounds like she is unhinged, too." Hawke said.

"Unhinged?" Böðvarsson asked.

"Her mind is messed up. Mental issues like Mari."

"Ahh, yes. He did mention that Rowena Albright attended the funeral. Paid for both the mother and daughter's burials. He didn't seem to know Wanza's condition. He said it was unfortunate that Wanza became sick and died. Which ultimately ate away at Mari."

Hawke nodded his head. "It seems Mari kept her daughter's condition a secret from everyone but her psychiatrist, and possibly Kanika."

"Who, if Mari hadn't contacted Rowena, must have filled her in when she came to the funeral." Böðvarsson drank his coffee and plucked a roll from the basket on the table. "I can question Rowena about the coat, since the act of trying to get rid of it, shows one of them wore it to get the rental car and leave the keys and note. However, I don't know how we can keep Kanika around. The coat belongs to Rowena. It will be tough proving the other woman wore it."

Hawke had his notes of the interview with Kanika in front of him. He'd been reading them as Böðvarsson mentioned his conversation with Kanika's superior. He glanced down at the photo of the woman delivering the keys to the hotel. Kanika had complained her feet were cold during the interview. He'd glanced down at her boots. That was why the ones in the photo looked familiar. "The hiking boots. They're Kanika's. She must have borrowed Rowena's coat with the big hood when she went back to get the car and when she was hiding from the surveillance cameras." He put the photos together along with the notes he'd written while interviewing the woman Wednesday evening. The time frame would fit for when she went back to get the rental car. It also made sense why she walked down to the mud pool asking if they could return to the bus. She'd put her boot prints at the scene in case the others were visible enough to trace. The woman had thought of everything.

"We need to bring her in for questioning, too. I think I've figured it out." Hawke leaned back as the waitress set his heaping plate of seafood on the table in front of him.

Böðvarsson picked up his utensils. "When we finish eating, I'll go to the office and request they come in for questioning." He glanced at Hawke. "Do you wish to come with me or go see your friend who arrived today?"

Hawke raised a forkful of white fish to his mouth.

"I think we can wait to pull them in until the morning. That will give us more time to pull everything together and give forensics some time to see if there is anything on the coat that will prove they killed Nonni."

"If you're going to the police station today, I'm going to walk around town," Dani said, as Hawke rose from the bed and dressed.

"That's a good idea. If you find something you want to go see close by, go. I'm sure I'm going to be busy all day." Hawke dropped a kiss on her head as he walked to the door. He'd told her when he'd returned the night before that he appreciated her not complaining about his being caught up in a murder. She'd said what he'd expected. "It is in you to seek justice. That is one of the traits I like about you." It was sappy, but it made his heart thump with pride and open even more toward the woman.

It was closer to two hours later when the taxi driver dropped him off. Hawke walked in through the front doors of the Hafnarfjörður police station.

The sergeant at the reception area motioned for him to come on through. "Detective Inspector Böðvarsson is waiting for you."

Hawke nodded and walked down the hall to the detective's office. The man was on the phone. He waved for Hawke to take a seat.

"Yes, I understand that your husband is arriving today. Yes. I would be willing to meet you at The Kvosin. And Kanika? Where might I catch up with her?" He frowned. "Thank you."

"You haven't had anyone bring them in yet?" Hawke asked.

"I arrived to find my commissioner wanting an update on the homicide. We have to visit Rowena at the Valkyrie suite at the Kvosin Hotel. She's moving there in preparation for her husband's arrival. I must get someone to catch Kanika at the airport." He picked his phone back up and spoke in Icelandic.

Hawke stood and paced the office. "She said she wasn't going home until Wednesday. Why did she change her mind?" Kanika had to be brought in before she got on the plane. Otherwise she could get lost in her own country once she returned.

Böðvarsson ended the call and stood, grabbing the car keys off the top of a pile of folders. "Come on. Perhaps we will have enough from Rowena to help build the case against Kanika when they bring her to the station." He picked up the case file folder.

Hawke followed the detective out the back of the station and into his sedan. The drive back toward downtown Reykjavik went faster than his trip to the station. Less than half an hour. Böðvarsson pulled up in front of an impressive four-story building that, while it was sided with metal, looked a bit like an old-time saloon and hotel. It had balconies on the middle section of the building and the square tops seen on old west buildings in the movies where the villains stood, waiting to shoot the good guys when they rode into town.

They entered the hotel. Böðvarsson walked straight to the elevators and up to the top floor. It was apparent he knew the Valkryie suite. He knocked on a door with the word Valkryie on a plaque beside the door.

Rowena answered the door. "Come in. Oh, and you brought the Yank cop." She smiled at Hawke and stepped aside.

He followed the detective into an open seating area that resembled a living room in a residence with large windows and a view of the downtown area. Rowena led them to a long dining room table with a sideboard along the inside wall and a row of windows, looking over roof tops and a view of a clock tower. This high up the view of the smattering of colorful roofs brightened the gloomy day.

"Please have a seat. I ordered coffee and biscuits. They should be arriv—" There was a knock on the door. "That must be them." She walked over to the apartment door.

Hawke followed Böðvarsson's lead and remained standing. He'd not dealt with royalty or shirttail royalty before, but it was plain the detective had.

Rowena and a hotel staff person returned.

"Would you like me to stay and serve?" the young woman asked.

"Not today, thank you." Rowena sat down at the end of the table.

The staff person let herself out.

Böðvarsson sat on Rowena's right. Hawke walked around and sat on her left.

The woman glanced at him as she placed a cup of coffee in front of him. "I hope you like coffee and biscuits."

He studied the baked goods on the tray. They looked like cookies to him. "We aren't here for you to entertain us."

She stared at him.

Böðvarsson cleared his throat. Hawke glanced his direction and received a frown.

"Mrs. Albright, as I said on the phone, we have some questions to ask you about the woman you roomed with at the conference." Böðvarsson pulled a curled file out of an inside pocket of his coat.

"Kanika? I don't know why you'd want to ask me questions about her. I met her when I went to my cousin's funeral in Machakos. When I learned she was coming to the conference, I thought it would be nice to room together. We could talk about Mari and perhaps heal from her unfortunate death." The woman sipped her coffee, glancing back and forth between Hawke and the detective.

"Did she ask to borrow your coat Wednesday evening?" Hawke asked.

Rowena studied him, sipped her coffee, and said, "She returned from her outing with your group, freezing, and said she was going to walk to a store and get something for her stomach. I offered my coat because it was much warmer than hers. My clothing is more suited to the weather here than anything she'd brought from Kenya."

"How long was she gone when she went to the store?" Böðvarsson asked.

Hawke was glad the detective was in sync with the questions he wanted answered.

"I can't tell you. I met some other Brits and we had drinks and talked until close to midnight. When I came in, she was in bed. My coat was hanging in the closet." She narrowed her eyes. "Why are you asking all of these questions?"

"And Friday? Did she ask to borrow your coat again?" Hawke asked instead of answering her question.

"I'm not sure. I know I wasn't wearing it. I was at the seminar I'd signed up to help with." She scowled at him. "Why are you asking these questions? Did Kanika do something wrong?"

"When you and Kanika talked about Mari, was Wanza brought up?" Böðvarsson asked.

"Wanza? What does she have to do with all of these questions?" The woman was starting to get angry.

Hawke glanced at the detective, he nodded, which Hawke took as meaning 'tell her what we know.'

"We believe Kanika came here to kill the young man who got Wanza pregnant." He decided not to say more than that and see how she responded.

Rowena leaned back in the chair, her gaze flitting back and forth between them. "You think Kanika killed that young man? Einar's son?"

"How did she seem when she talked about Mari and Wanza?" Böðvarsson asked again, more gently.

"She talked of Mari as if she had loved her like a sister. They had been close as police partners and spent a lot of time together. She talked a little about Wanza. Mostly that she had broken Mari's heart when she'd planned to move to Iceland and go to school."

"Did she tell you that Mari forced Wanza to have an abortion and that was what killed her?" Hawke didn't believe in being subtle when trying to find a murderer.

The woman gasped and stared at him. "Why would she force Wanza to do something so horrible? Who was the father? Wouldn't he have helped with the baby and perhaps married her?"

"I believe he would have, had he known about the pregnancy." The pain he'd seen in Bragi's eyes when they'd talked about Wanza, he was pretty sure the young man would have married her, and they would have been happy. Instead three lives had been lost by a mother's misguided beliefs.

"Wanza didn't tell him?" Rowena appeared perplexed.

"She'd stopped all correspondence with him three months after she left the conference two years ago." Hawke watched the woman. She appeared as unsettled as anyone would learning all of this news about a family member.

"And the young man who was killed, was he the father?" She studied him closely.

Hawke had a feeling she hadn't killed Nonni, but he didn't want to give away the real father in case she was in this with Kanika. "No, he wasn't."

She sighed and shook her head. "Kanika's revenge wasn't even on the right person."

"Correct. We need to get enough proof she did this to hold her for his murder. If she learns she killed the wrong person, she may try again." Böðvarsson slid the photos of the woman leaving the messages at the two hotels and getting into the taxi in front of Rowena. "Does that look like your coat?"

She picked each one up and studied it closely. "I can't be certain but it looks like it." She set the photo down and pointed to the person. "You think that is Kanika?"

Hawke pointed to the hiking shoes. "Do those look like her shoes?"

Rowena leaned down and studied them. "They could be. Again, I couldn't prove it, but they look similar." She tapped the photo taken in the Center

Hotel. "What is she doing? This one isn't our hotel."

"That is my hotel. She was leaving a note for me, trying to put me onto someone else as the killer." Hawke studied the woman. She seemed to take that in and didn't say anything.

"And here? She told me she walked to a store, why is she getting in a taxi?"

"She took that back to Krýsuvík to get the rental car she 'borrowed' back to the owner." Böðvarsson emphasized borrowed enough that the woman's gaze latched onto him.

"By borrow you're saying she stole it?"

"She returned the keys. That is the photo of her at your hotel." Hawke decided to tell a bit more and see if she could shed a light. "Tuesday night when a gathering of several ladies were in Kevin Largess's room at the hotel, Kanika took the keys to his rental car. I don't know if he made a comment about not going anywhere until Saturday and she figured he wouldn't even miss the car or she was just being bold and decided that was better than stealing or renting a car to take her to Krýsuvík and follow Nonni."

"Did you happen to see her take the keys or have them in her possession on Tuesday night or Wednesday morning?" Böðvarsson asked.

Rowena sipped her coffee, picked up a cookie and nibbled on it, and then her eyes widened. "She did spill a glass of water when we were in Kevin's room. It was on the glass case with all the fishing gear. I remember there being keys on it when I watched her wipe up the mess, but that's all." She nibbled the cookie some more. "And Wednesday, I asked her why she was leaving so early when the schedule said the workshop with you didn't start until nine. She said she wanted to talk with someone."

Hawke glanced at Böðvarsson, taking notes. He was getting it all down.

"Did you or Kanika go to the bar in Harpa on Tuesday night? Maybe after you left Kevin's?" Hawke wondered how Kanika had figured out Nonni was the person he'd planned to track.

"No. We went back to our room and went to sleep." Rowena poured more coffee in all of their cups from the carafe the staff person had brought up with the tray.

Discovering how Kanika knew Nonni was being tracked would help them connect her to the homicide.

"I need to go," Hawke said, pushing his chair back from the table.

"Isn't there more you need to ask me?" Rowena put her cup of coffee down and stared at him.

He had a feeling she thought by detaining them, she was allowing Kanika the freedom to get out of Iceland. That was a mistake on her part. Hawke glanced at Bodversson. From the frown on his forehead, he'd presumed she was in cahoots with the murderer as well. If she was hindering them to keep the woman from getting caught, she knew what Kanika was up to. And they had given her almost all of their evidence to the killing.

Hawke stood. "I'm sure Detective Inspector Böðvarsson can ask you the rest of the questions." When she rose, he added, "I can let myself out."

Böðvarsson nodded.

Hawke took that to mean he would ask more questions and continue with whatever he needed to do.

At the door, he stepped out and listened. They were speaking too low for him to hear. He was sure, Böðvarsson would push to get more specifics on what they had already questioned her about.

Right now, he wanted to talk to Riku and see if she remembered seeing Kanika in the restaurant Wednesday morning when she and Nonni met. The woman had to have overheard that he was going to be the one tracked.

On the street, walking toward the Marina Hotel, he dialed Riku.

"Hello, Mr. Hawke," she answered.

"Riku are you at your hotel?"

"Yes."

"I'll be there in ten minutes. I have some more questions I need to ask."

"Okay. Father and I will be in lobby."

"Thanks." Hawke hung up and received a text from Dani.

I'm taking a tour bus around the Golden Circle. Have fun. I hope to have this finished by tonight. See you then.

He loved that Dani understood duty. Her career in the Air Force had taught her there were things that had to be done before anything else. Few women he knew understood that.

Stepping into the lobby of the Marina Hotel, he spotted Riku and Mr. Tanaka immediately. They both stood as he approached.

"Have you figured out who killed Nonni?" Riku asked.

"I can't tell you who we are looking at, but can you remember Wednesday morning when you met Nonni, who else was sitting near you in the restaurant?"

She scrunched her face and thought.

"It would have had to have been close enough they overheard him tell you he was being tracked for my class." Hawke glanced at Mr. Tanaka. He studied his daughter. He held her in great esteem. His love shone in his eyes and the slight grimace of his lips as he willed his daughter to find the truth.

Hawke had a feeling the man had been as grieved over Nonni's death as his daughter.

Her eyes opened and she gasped. "I don't remember who was around us, but we took a selfie." She pulled out her phone and began flipping through the photos. She stopped and tears glistened in the corner of her eyes. "Here it is."

Hawke studied the two. They had been in love. There is a glow when two people have found their soulmates. It was shining bright in the couple's smiles and eyes. He studied the photo beyond the couple. Bingo! "Can you text that photo to me, please?"

She went through the motions and his phone buzzed. The picture opened in his text messages.

"Thank you. This will help us." He faced Mr. Tanaka. "Are you going home today?"

"No, we will remain for Nonni's funeral service. Riku wishes to pay her last respects." His sad eyes met his daughter's.

"If it happens this week, let me know. I'm not leaving until Saturday." He shook hands with Mr. Tanaka and patted Riku on the shoulder.

With the picture he now had in his possession, they had a way to play the cousin against the friend and get the truth about Nonni's death.

Chapter Twenty-five

Outside the Marina Hotel, Hawke called Böðvarsson.

"Where did you go?" the detective asked.

"To get more proof against Rowena and Kanika. And I have it. Where are you?" Hawke stood at the spot waiting to be picked up by a taxi.

"Leaving the hotel. I can pick you up."

"Marina Hotel." He stepped away from the taxi pickup as a car pulled up. He shook his head and wandered twenty feet away, pulling the collar of his coat up and dunking his head down to keep the cold wind from blowing in his ears. He should have put his stocking cap on this morning instead of his Stetson. He'd better remember that this week while he and Dani were sightseeing.

Böðvarsson pulled up to the curb. Before Hawke was settled in the seat he asked, "What did you get?"

Hawke held up his phone with the photo. "This

was Wednesday morning when Nonni told Riku he was helping me. My class description said we were going to track a person. The person who overheard Nonni and Riku's conversation had to have already been following Nonni to figure out their best chance of getting him alone."

"I don't like this." Böðvarsson stared at the photo. "There could be an explanation for her being in the restaurant beyond following him."

Hawke studied the detective. "Getting cold feet because of who she is?"

"A little. If we have this wrong, I could be demoted for having brought scandal to our country." Böðvarsson pulled away from the curb.

"Have they picked up Kanika?"

"She is at the police station." Böðvarsson headed the vehicle south.

"I say we play the information we have off of each of them. We have the photo of Rowena overhearing the conversation, relaying that to Kanika, who follows him in the car that Rowena told us Kanika stole the keys to—"

"Wait a minute. She didn't tell us that Kanika stole the keys." Böðvarsson stared at him as they waited for a light to change.

"She all but handed us Kanika on a platter, saying how she spilled water and the keys were laying there." Hawke snapped his fingers. "I'll call Sigga and see if she remembers the water spilling."

He found the woman's number and dialed.

"Halló?" the Chief Inspector answered.

"This is Hawke. Are you back to work today?"

"Oh, hello. No. I don't work until Wednesday.

Why?"

"Where are you? I have a question about the other night at Largess's I need to ask."

"Which night?" she said suspiciously.

"Tuesday night when the gaggle of women were in his room."

"I told you I wasn't there very long when the other women were."

"Are you still at the hotel?" he asked.

"Just getting ready to check out."

"Are there any other women there who were in the room that night? If so, gather them in the lobby and I'll be right there." He hung up and found Böðvarsson turning around.

"What was that about?"

"We'll see who else remembers the water spilling."

"What will that prove?" the detective asked.

"It will prove either more people saw her messing with the top of the counter, or her partner in crime is tossing her to the sharks because she has more political pull." Hawke slipped his phone back into his coat pocket.

They pulled up to the doors of the hotel.

Böðvarsson showed his badge and asked the valet to watch his car. Inside the doors, they found Sigga, Carmilla, and Mayta.

"What's this about, Hawke?" Mayta asked.

"Tuesday night when you were all in Kevin Largess's room. Do you remember anyone spilling water?"

They all glanced at one another.

"We were drinking wine," Carmilla said.

"And I arrived just before the party broke up,"

Sigga added.

"Okay, did anyone spill their wine?" he asked.

They again glanced at one another and shook their heads.

"You don't remember anyone spilling anything that night?" Böðvarsson asked.

"No," Carmilla said.

"And you were all in the room the whole time together?" Hawke asked.

Carmilla glared at Sigga. "We all left but her. She was alone with Kevin."

"Thank you, ladies. We appreciate you taking time to talk to us." Hawke pivoted and headed for the door.

In the car, Böðvarsson asked. "What did that prove?"

"That Rowena is throwing Kanika under the bus for this homicide."

"Because Kanika did it or because Rowena did it?" Böðvarsson pulled out into traffic and they were on their way to the police station this time.

"My guess is, Rowena planned it all and Kanika executed it." Hawke stared out the window wondering how they were going to get the grief-stricken cousin to put her own neck in the noose.

Hawke followed Böðvarsson into an interview room at the police station. If looks could kill, he and the Icelandic detective would have turned to ash from the glare they received.

"Why did you bring me to the police station?" Kanika asked.

Böðvarsson started a recording. "Will you please state your name and where you live?"

She continued glaring but recited her name and address. She repeated, "Why did you bring me here?"

"We have evidence that says you are the person who killed Jón Einarsson, also called Nonni," Böðvarsson stated.

She pressed her lips so tight together, Hawke wondered if a crowbar would get them apart.

Böðvarsson opened up the worn file. He placed the information about her working with Mari, her trip to the shrink, how she asked for vacation time, and paid for the trip on her own, on the table, facing her.

"We know you and Mari Odeyna were partners on the Machakos Police. That you and she spent a lot of time together. We believe she told you that Wanza, her daughter, was pregnant and going to leave her. She didn't want to lose her daughter and forced her to get an abortion."

Hawke studied the woman as Böðvarsson laid out what they had pieced together. Her lips remained locked, her eyes bore between their two heads and into the wall behind them. Tears glistened in the corners of her eyes, the only sign she was listening to a word he said.

She sobbed when the detective mentioned Wanza dying as a result of the abortion and Mari killing herself out of guilt.

"And all you and Mari talked about was how it was the young man's fault who took advantage of young Wanza." Hawke drew her attention to him.

"She was only seventeen when she come here. She should not have gone to bars or slept with anyone. She was a good girl before she come to Iceland." The woman's emotions finally burst forth. "He should not have taken advantage of her!"

"Who?" Hawke asked.

"Nonni, the man who made her pregnant and talked her into moving here. He did not know what was best for her. Her mother know best." Kanika's eyes were wide with rage. Her face darker than usual.

"You killed the wrong man." Hawke watched her.

She narrowed her eyes. "I did not say I killed anyone."

"Aren't you curious though? I just said you killed the wrong man. You thought the father of Wanza's child was Nonni. I happen to know it wasn't."

Kanika glared at him, but he could see she was thinking behind that glare.

"I'm not positive it was you who killed him," Böðvarsson said, as if he were trying to be the good cop. "But Mrs. Albright says she saw you take the rental car keys from Kevin Largess's hotel room on Tuesday night. And we have surveillance film of either you or her returning the keys to the hotel desk Wednesday night."

"She wouldn't say I took the keys. You are lying to me." Kanika stared at them.

Böðvarsson pulled out his notepad that he'd scribbled in while Rowena talked this morning. "We visited Mrs. Albright at her suite in the Kvosin Hotel. She said 'She did spill a glass of water when we were in Kevin's room. It was on the glass case with all the fishing gear. I remember there being keys on it when I watched her wipe up the mess.' The her and she Mrs. Albright is talking about is you."

Hawke plunged in. "According to the other women who were in the room, nothing was spilled. She lied to make you look guilty."

Kanika's head moved slightly back and forth as if she were evaluating what she'd heard and if she really thought the other woman had sold her out. "I don't believe she said that. Why would she try to say I killed him? I didn't even know him."

"But you hated him for hurting Wanza, taking her away from Mari, and Mari taking her own life," Hawke said softly.

"Yes, I hated the man who preyed on the sweet girl and caused my friend to make bad choices. What would killing him do? It wouldn't bring back Wanza and Mari." She stared at him.

He was on the fence about whether or not she'd killed Nonni. She'd worked hard at covering her tracks, and she'd stared him straight in the eyes when she said what a sane person would say.

Hawke pulled Böðvarsson's file over in front of him and pulled out the photos of the woman in the coat and hiking boots. "This is Rowena's coat, you borrowed—her words—on Wednesday night when you picked up the rental car at Krýsuvík and returned the keys to the registration desk at the Marina Hotel. You also wore this coat when you left a note, trying to deflect me to another person, at my hotel."

"That is Rowena's coat. It's not me."

Hawke pointed to the hiking boots. "Those are the boots you had on when we spoke right after we all came back from Krýsuvík. I remember looking at them when you complained your feet were cold. When you said your feet were cold, I put it off to the warm climate you came from. But if you followed Nonni, killed him, walked back to the parking lot, waited for the bus to arrive and fell in with the rest of the participants, walked back to where we found the body and back to the bus, your feet would be colder and wetter than the others."

She didn't glance at him while he talked, only stared at the photo in front of her.

"Had you planned to drive the car back after our tracking or had leaving it there been the plan all along?" Hawke had wondered about that. If no one noticed she was missing on the bus to the parking lot, would they have noticed her missing on the way back when they were busy talking about the body and how the class was cut short?

"I would like a lawyer." She sat back in her chair and crossed her arms.

Böðvarsson turned off the recording and gathered his photos and papers into the file. "I'll see what I can find." He stood and walked to the door.

Hawke remained at the table, studying the woman. Had she killed Nonni? Or was she being loyal to the person who would have more money and pull? "You do know, the courts will be harder on you than Rowena if she is found guilty. If you are covering for her, you'd do yourself a favor by telling your lawyer and us the truth."

She flicked a glance his direction and remained silent.

Rising out of the chair, he thumped his knuckles on the table, making her jump. "We will discover which one of you killed Nonni. I found the coat you two shoved in the ice crevice. It's at forensics now."

Kanika gasped then hid the surprise.

"When we get that and fill in all the blanks, we'll

make sure you or Rowena get the maximum sentence. Nonni didn't deserve to die. All he did was help Wanza find a way to go to college here. The same thing he would have done for anyone who wished to go to school in Iceland."

Chapter Twenty-six

Sitting in Böðvarsson's office, Hawke kept running what they knew over and over in his head. "There has to be a way to discover which one of them actually killed him. We can push that it was Kanika and I think the evidence would bear it out to get her convicted, but if we pushed her through and then discovered it was really Rowena who committed the crime, we would have done an injustice to Kanika."

Böðvarsson nodded. "We have to either make Kanika tell us how Rowena did it, or orchestrated it, or get her to tell us she did it." He flipped through the pages of typed notes. "I think I'll give Dr. Mutambe a call and see if he has any suggestions on what might trigger Kanika to tell us the truth."

"That's a good idea. I'm going to reread the forensic reports." Hawke picked up his pack. "I'll be down the hall in the break room."

Böðvarsson nodded as he flipped through the pages of his folder.

Out in the hall, Hawke headed to the breakroom, but it took him right by the room where an officer stood, guarding Kanika. He nodded and started to open the door, but decided he needed to have new ammunition before he talked to her anymore.

In the breakroom, he texted Dani. *Are you having fun?*

She didn't respond. That meant she was busy, hopefully, enjoying herself.

He pulled the file out of his pack and opened it. Digging through the papers, he found all three of the forensic reports. He started with the first initial report. At the scene, the coroner had said, it appeared to be blunt force trauma to the back of the head. He skipped to the third report talking about the rock they found with blood and hair from the victim. It was 3.63 kilograms.

Hawke pulled out his phone and googled what that would be in pounds. Close to 8 pounds. Not too heavy, but still it would take added force to strike someone hard enough with that weight to knock them out. Unless he landed face first in the pool. Then the shock and a well-placed foot would have kept him under until he suffocated.

The second report stated there was brown fluid in the sphenoid sinuses, and edematous/boggy lungs with aspirated bog fluid.

Hawke went back to the rock. He picked up his phone. It buzzed in his hand. Dani.

I'm walking around Gullfoss. It's a beautiful waterfall. The people are all friendly and speak such

*good English, I don't feel like I'm in another country.
Will I see you soon?*

*Unsure. We have our murderer but getting her to
talk is another thing. I'll let you know if I can meet for
dinner.*

Sounds good. Good luck!

Thanks.

He read the message again and smiled.
Experiencing more of Iceland with Dani was going to
be a trip he wouldn't soon forget.

Glancing at the forensic report, he found a phone
number and put the call through.

"Hállo," and then he didn't understand what the
woman said.

"Hello, I'm State Trooper Hawke working with
Detective Inspector Böðvarsson on the Jon Einarson
case. I would like to talk to Halla. I have a question."

"Oh yes, I can put you through to her lab."

The phone made some clicks and another female
voice answered. "Hawke, how may I help you?"

"We think we have the person who killed the mud
pool victim. But I have a question. From where the
victim was struck on the head, can you tell how tall the
attacker might have been?" There was a good four to
five inches difference in Rowena and Kanika's height.
Which, now that he thought about it, would help them
tell who was wearing the coat.

The woman came back on the line. "My
researchers figure it would have been someone slightly
shorter than the victim. The blow was lower on the
back of the head than if it had been by someone taller.
Does that help?"

Hawke smiled. They had her. "Yes. Can you send

that in writing over to Detective Inspector Böðvarsson?"

"Yes, I can."

"Thank you." Hawke stood and walked back to Böðvarsson's office. "We have her."

Böðvarsson put the phone back on the cradle. "What did you come up with?"

"Looking at the forensic files I wondered where the rock struck the victim on the head. And according to Halla, the assailant had to have been a few inches shorter than the victim. That would be Kanika. I would say Rowena is a couple inches taller than Nonni." He tapped the folder with his finger. "And we should check the photos of the person wearing the coat. The photos show the same shoes, but I believe in the photo where the message was being left for me, the coat bottom is higher up on the wearer's legs."

Böðvarsson pulled the photos out. "You're right. Rowena left the note for you. But why would she try to incriminate Sigga?"

"I think she was just trying to get us to look somewhere else, but we hadn't even started looking into Kanika." Hawke put his hand on the doorknob. "Ready to see if we can get her to break?"

Böðvarsson shook his head. "She asked for a lawyer, we have to wait for one to show up. In the meantime, I've filled the prosecutor in on what we think. Kanika did the killing but Rowena Albright was also mixed up in it."

"Did the shrink in Kenya give you any help with how to get to the truth with Kanika?" Hawke asked, moving to the chair by the detective's desk.

"He said, she is stubborn. We're either going to

have to play on her sense of justice, why she became a policewoman or get her mad to where she just starts barking back and not thinking about what she's saying."

Hawke liked the first way better, but had a feeling her sense of justice had been skewed since she'd killed a person to, in her mind, get justice for the mother and daughter. "Then I guess we follow the path that she gravitates toward." His stomach growled. "Any chance we have time to grab something to eat?"

The detective smiled. "That's a good idea." He stood and walked into the hall. Stopping at the officer still standing in the hall outside the room where Kanika sat, he said, "Call me when her lawyer arrives."

The officer nodded.

Hawke followed the detective down the hall and out the back of the building.

"You're in for a treat. My favorite place has seafood soup today." Böðvarsson slid behind the wheel of his car and Hawke settled into the passenger seat. He liked fish and was curious about the seafood soup.

Hawke leaned back in the chair. The small restaurant had known Böðvarsson when he walked through the door and gave them a nice table in the corner away from the other patrons. The soup and bread were delicious. The mussels were still in the shell in the soup, but he didn't mind digging for the meat. The broth was creamy with a hint of tomato.

"That's an Icelandic lunch," Böðvarsson said, raising a glass of beer.

Hawke had refrained from beer this early in the day. He picked up his cup of coffee. "I've never had soup like that before. It was better than I thought it would be when you mentioned it."

The detective laughed. "We eat a lot of fish and lamb. And vegetables. The geothermal heat is used in hothouses."

"I'm excited to explore more of your country this week. My friend has arrived. I'm sure she is mapping out our routes."

Böðvarsson's eyebrows raised. "She? Then it is a woman who you are spending time with this week?"

Hawke grinned. "Who did you think I'd spend my time with?"

"Sigga suggested you were not interested in women."

Hawke laughed. "Because I didn't jump into bed with her."

"I told her I thought maybe you just weren't into one-night flings."

"True." Hawke finished off his coffee. "I can't believe Kanika hasn't found a lawyer by now. I would have thought Rowena would have supplied her with one. If they are friends."

The corners of Böðvarsson's eyes crinkled. "She has a lawyer. I was texted halfway through our meal. I wanted to give them time to talk and see if maybe he would talk sense into her and she would admit to killing Nonni with Rowena's help."

"Good thinking. Let's go see."

Chapter Twenty-seven

"What are the charges against my client?" the short bald-headed man sitting next to Kanika asked as soon as Hawke and Böðvarsson entered the room.

The detective had stopped in his office long enough to pick up the information Halla had sent over and the arrest warrant the prosecutor had sent over. He slid the arrest warrant across the table to the lawyer.

The man read it and shook his head. "Ms. Tumaini says she didn't kill this man."

"We have proof she did," Böðvarsson said, sliding the forensic report across the table.

Again, the man read it. He shoved it back. "That is nothing more than a forensic report. Anyone could have hit the victim on the head with a rock."

Kanika flinched at the man's comment.

Hawke didn't know if Böðvarsson saw it, but it meant she didn't want to relive the moment. One that he was sure was pushed by Rowena. If he could just get her to see that the other woman had driven her to do the unspeakable. He had a thought.

"Kanika, did Rowena call you on the anniversary of her cousin's death?" Hawke waved away Böðvarsson's throat clearing.

"What does this have to do with the charges against my client?" the lawyer's forehead was beading with sweat.

It was a clue that the lawyer was working for the Albrights. "I'm wondering if Rowena didn't bring up the idea of settling the score then and talked your client into taking her vacation this past week and signing up for the conference so the two of them could get their revenge for Mari and Wanza." Hawke didn't look at the lawyer. He kept his gaze on Kanika. She didn't look up from her clenched hands on the table.

"I think she masterminded all of this and now that you've been caught, she's planning to have you take the fall for all of it." Hawke leaned across the table, catching the woman's gaze. "Rowena left Kenya as a child. She didn't really know her cousin like you did. You worked side by side with Mari, enforcing the law. Do you think she would have condoned what you've done? She was so grieved over her daughter's death— something that could have been avoided had Mari been thinking straight—that she took her life. But she didn't take the life of the young man who had loved her daughter—still loves her. He doesn't know she's dead. He tried to locate her, but couldn't."

Kanika stared in his eyes now. "I tried to tell her that maybe it would be good for Wanza to get out of Kenya. Times are not good for women. Mari and I tried

236

to show her that you didn't have to be less worthy than a man. Mari feared that was how the man here would treat Wanza. Use the child to keep her lowly."

Hawke shook his head. "She would have been loved, respected, and taken care of. That I'm sure of having met the young man. I only wish Mari would have allowed Wanza to reach out to him. Many lives would have been saved."

Tears trickled down the woman's face. "It is as you say. Rowena was angry when I told her about Wanza and how it ate at Mari and she took her life. She asked me who the man was. I told her I did not know."

The lawyer put a hand on her arm. "They don't have enough to prove you did anything. You should not say anymore."

She shook his hand off. "I am an officer of the law. I know I have broken the law and wish to tell my story." Kanika shifted her gaze to Böðvarsson. "Is the recording going?"

He nodded.

"It was on the anniversary of Mari's death that Rowena contacted me. She began talking about Mari and her death and how it was the man's fault we lost Mari and Wanza. She suggested we come to the conference and find out who the man was and confront him. That was what she said, confront him." Kanika licked her lips. "May I have some water?"

Böðvarsson rose, opened the door, and spoke to the officer. He returned.

She continued, "When I arrived, Rowena said she had found the man. His name was Nonni. She pointed him out as we stood in line to register. He had a young Asian woman talking to him. They were laughing and holding hands. I said, 'He is going to get another girl in trouble.' Rowena fed this anger in me. She said we had to stop him before he ruined another woman's life.'"

A slight knock on the door interrupted the woman. An officer entered with a glass of water. He handed it to Böðvarsson who placed it in front of Kanika.

She thanked the officer, who left the room, and drank about a third of the glass before continuing.

"Tuesday night, when we were in Kevin's room, Rowena told me to take the keys after Kevin made the comment he would not be able to go anywhere until Friday night. Later in our room, she said we could use the car to follow Nonni. She was up and gone when I awoke Wednesday morning. But she called me and said to get ready for the hiking part of your class, bring the car keys, and meet her in the hotel restaurant. She told me she overheard Nonni saying he was the person who was going to be tracked. She said that was the best time to get him alone and seek revenge." She put her hands over her face, scrubbed her cheeks, and sighed. "I followed him to the parking lot, waited to see which way he went, then kept my distance. But I lost sight of him and not wanting to leave my prints near his, I wandered around, until I came to the mud pool. He was already in the pool when I found him. Seeing him lying there, knowing I'd followed him, I knew if I said anything, you would think I killed him. I hurried back to the parking lot in a wider angle than before. I returned about ten minutes before the bus arrived. I waited until it stopped and walked behind it, joining everyone as they got off." She stared in Hawke's eyes. "I did not kill him. But I realize now that Rowena's suggestions of returning for the car, rather than having

Kevin call it in as stolen, returning the keys, it all makes me look guilty."

Hawke had watched the woman as she told her story. He believed her that she didn't kill Nonni. But he had a feeling that Rowena did. Why else would she have set Kanika up? Perhaps she believed Kanika could have done more to save her cousin?

Leaning back in the chair, Hawke crossed his arms and peered into the woman's eyes. "I believe you. But I still think Rowena has something to do with it. Did you see anyone in the car with Nonni?"

"No. And I did not see anyone else walking. There was just the two of us."

Hawke had another question for the woman. "Why did you try to hide the coat in the glacier?"

The woman's eyes widened. "You found it?"

"Yes. Why the glacier and not just chuck it into the harbor?" Hawke could see she was also wondering that.

"Rowena told me to bring it. When she saw the crack, she said she would keep you busy while I shoved the coat into the crack." She shook her head. "On the drive back, I realized she did that to make me look more guilty."

Hawke nodded.

Kanika shifted her gaze to Böðvarsson. "I did not kill Nonni. I am only guilty of not contacting the police when I found the body and being coerced into doing things I would not normally do."

The detective nodded. "We'll worry about that later. But I think, since Rowena wants you to be accused, we'll keep you here, not under arrest but to keep her thinking her plan has worked." Böðvarsson narrowed his eyes at the lawyer. "Are you also the lawyer for Mrs. Albright?"

The man nodded his head.

"I'll have to detain you to keep you from contacting her." Böðvarsson held out his hand. "Your phone please."

"I have other clients that might need my services," the lawyer argued.

"You can remain in this room with Ms. Tumaini or you can be booked for aiding in a homicide. Which would you rather it be?" Böðvarsson's hand remained palm up over the table.

The lawyer placed his phone on the upturned hand.

"You will both be allowed to leave, when we have what we need on Mrs. Albright and the person who killed Nonni." Böðvarsson picked up the files.

Hawke followed him to the door and spun back to the room. "You wanted us to know the truth. That's why you told me you rode to the mud pools with Mari, your dead friend. You were giving me a clue to why Nonni was dead."

Kanika nodded.

"But why did you continue to let Rowena tell you to do all the other things, like the note and leaving the coat?"

She shrugged. "She has a strong personality that is hard to disobey."

Hawke stepped out of the room.

"*Helvítis*! I thought we had the murderer," Böðvarsson said, shoving his door open and dropping the files on the desk.

Hawke dropped into the chair in front of the desk. "It has to be someone who knew where Nonni was going." He thought back to when he talked to Nonni.

"His friends, Ásta, Katrín, and Bragi were there. He could have told them…" He thought about the three and the way they had behaved around Nonni. They had all seemed like genuine friends. What was it Einar had said, he thought Nonni was going to ask Ásta to marry him. But it was clear that Nonni and Riku were in love.

"We need to recheck the time line for Ásta and Billy on Wednesday." He pulled the file to him and started reading the information.

"Why those two?" Böðvarsson asked.

"Because they are the only two who really had a problem with Nonni. Billy because of the defamation of his father, and Ásta because Nonni was in love with Riku."

"I'm confused. Then where does Mrs. Albright fit into all of this?" Böðvarsson sat in his chair and stared at Hawke.

"Right in the middle."

Chapter Twenty-eight

Hawke held Kanika's recorded interview in his hands. "Right here. If we believe Kanika that she found the body, returned to the parking lot, and waited ten minutes for the bus to arrive, that means Nonni was killed between ten and ten-thirty. That would have been plenty of time for Billy to get back to town and pick up Ásta for lunch."

"He said he drove Ásta number two's car there to meet Nonni at three and saw the police cars." Böðvarsson shuffled through the pages in his folder.

Hawke paced the room, thinking. "Did he pick up Ásta for lunch from work?"

Böðvarsson plucked a paper from the file. "That's what it says."

"Where does she work?" They had to find a hole in their story.

"A dress shop in the Kringlan shopping center." Böðvarsson stood. "Would you like to buy your friend a dress?"

Hawke grinned. "I think I would."

On the drive to the shopping center, Böðvarsson explained the center was just off a freeway that headed south.

In the store, they asked to speak to the manager. She was a tall, thin, gray-haired woman of about sixty.

"How may I help the police?" she asked.

"We were wondering if you could tell us what time Ásta came in to work on Wednesday last?" Böðvarsson asked.

The woman marched to the back of the counter and began tapping on the computer. "She called in sick that day. We didn't see her until Friday. Is she in trouble? I only hire young men and women who aren't in trouble in any way."

"We are just clarifying things. Do you happen to know if she comes to work in a car or rides the bus?" Böðvarsson asked.

"I believe she has a car. Though she mostly rides the bus to work." The woman studied them both. "I know the young man who was killed last week was a friend of hers. She was devastated when she came to work on Friday."

"Thank you. You've been helpful." Böðvarsson pointed to a bright blue dress. "Would your friend like that one?"

Hawke shook his head. "She's more a jeans and overalls person."

Böðvarsson grinned. "I hope you will introduce us."

Walking out of the store, Hawke had a feeling the detective would have them pulled over just so he could meet Dani.

In the car, Hawke said, "It sounds to me like we need to ask Billy and Ásta to come into the station for an interview." A thought struck him. "If Ásta was working with Rowena, and I told her that Nonni wasn't the father of her niece's child…" He pulled out his phone. "I need to call Bragi." He didn't have the young man's number but he had Katrín's.

"Hello? Hawke do you need more information?" Katrín answered.

"I need Bragi's phone number," he said without preamble.

"He's right here, would you like to talk with him?"

"Yes. Thank you."

Hawke listened close as the phone was being passed. There were voices and the sound of dishes in the background. They were some place public.

"Hello? Hawke?" Bragi answered.

"Hi Bragi. I have some news I'd like to tell you about Wanza. Could you come to the police station?"

"What have you found? Is she well?" The excitement in his voice put a lump in Hawke's throat.

"I'll tell you when you get here. And don't talk to anyone about this. Not Katrín or any of your friends. Just come to the police station."

"I don't understand?" He said something in Icelandic.

"Don't say a word and come straight to the police station." He ended the connection. "Man, I hope he does what I asked."

"Is he coming to the station?" Böðvarsson asked.

"Yes, but I hope he keeps it to himself. If he starts talking about Wanza and Rowena hears, I fear he may end up dead." Hawke sat and stewed on that the rest of the way to the station.

When they arrived, an angry Billy Weston was being led into the building. "What the hell is going on?" he demanded, seeing Hawke.

"We have some more questions for you," Hawke hurried into the building and wasn't surprised to see that Bragi had beat them to the station. "Come back with me."

The young man followed him down the hall to the interview room. When they were both seated Hawke stared into the hopeful face of the young man. While Bragi knew English well, Hawke wasn't sure he could convey everything to him in a foreign language.

"Just a minute." Hawke stepped into the hall. Böðvarsson was closing a door on the other interview room. "Weston?"

"Yes. Want help?"

Hawke nodded.

Böðvarsson followed him into the room where Bragi's nerves had the air vibrating.

"Something bad has happened, hasn't it?" he said, his hands were clenched together on top of the table.

"I'm not sure where to start." Hawke wanted the young man to be aware his life was in danger if they didn't get Rowena as an accomplice to Nonni's death. But he also knew the young man may not listen to that until he'd heard the news about Wanza.

"Do you wish me to tell him?" Böðvarsson asked.

"No, just jump in if he doesn't understand the English words." Hawke started with knowing that Nonni had been helping Wanza to come back here to go to school and live with Bragi.

"Yes. We only knew each other for a week but it

felt as if we'd known one another all our lives. I don't understand why she stopped talking with me." He glanced back and forth between them.

Hawke swallowed the lump in his throat and began, "She'd discovered she was pregnant."

The young man's eyes widened before he glared. "Who was the father?"

"You."

Bragi's glare turned to pride and a smile split his face. "I am a father! Why does she not tell me?"

Hawke shook his head. "Because her mother made her get an abortion and Wanza lost her life from that procedure."

The young man deflated before Hawke's eyes. All the excitement, pride, and life seemed to drain out of him. "How could a mother do such a thing?"

"We'll never know why her mother had such strong feelings for Wanza having a child or moving to Iceland. But a month after Wanza's death, her mother killed herself—over guilt, remorse, pain, we'll never know for sure."

The young man cried, he wiped at the tears with fists and asked, "Why did you not want me to tell anyone?"

"Because we believe Nonni was killed, because a relative of Wanza's wished the father of her baby dead."

"But Nonni wasn't the father. I was. I don't understand?" Bragi glanced between the two.

"The person who orchestrated Nonni's death thought he was the father because of all the emails he sent Wanza about moving here." Hawke watched as the realization dawned on the young man.

"Nonni was killed because of me?" His eyes teared up again. "He was my best friend. He worked with Wanza for me, because he had more contacts."

"Not just because of you. I also believe that someone used Wanza's relative as a way to kill Nonni." Hawke had been piecing it all together.

Bragi shook his head. "I don't understand."

"When we have the murderers locked up, we will tell you all, but first, you must remain somewhere you feel safe and no one other than your family can see you until we say we have caught the person," Böðvarsson said.

"Family? Why must I stay with family?" Bragi stared at Böðvarsson.

Hawke motioned for the man to tell him in their language. While they were speaking, Hawke texted Dani. *I'll be late getting in tonight, but should be done with this case by then.*

She sent him a thumbs up emoji.

"Do you understand?" Böðvarsson said as Bragi nodded his head. "We'll have a policeman escort you to your parent's house."

"And don't call Katrín or Sindri until we call you," Hawke added.

"What about Ásta?" Bragi asked.

"Definitely not her." Hawke stood.

Bragi stood, but stared at Hawke. "She had something to do with Nonni's death, didn't she?"

"Why do you ask?" Hawke was interested in hearing what the young man had to say.

"That night, Wednesday, she's the one who told us Nonni was dead. She looked right at Riku when she said it, like she wanted to hurt her." He shrugged. "At the time, I just thought it was her trying to blame Riku, but I think she was trying to make her hurt more."

"It was both. Remember, go to your family and don't talk to anyone." Hawke patted Bragi on the back as he exited the room.

Böðvarsson and Hawke entered the room where Billy Weston had been waiting.

"You know I get a lawyer, right?" Billy sneered at Böðvarsson.

"You don't need a lawyer, we're just asking a few questions about Wednesday and when you and Ásta, the one without the red hair and inner thigh birthmark, really went to Krýsuvík." Hawke sat down across from the angry young man.

"I told you. We had lunch, fooled around, and I kept my meeting with Nonni, only there were police cars, so I left." Billy leaned back in his chair and crossed his arms.

"I'm talking about before you used Ásta's, with the red hair and birthmark, car to go to the parking lot. I mean when Ásta, with the brown hair, picked you up in her car and you drove out to Lake Kleifarvatn. You followed a dirt road at the south end of the lake where you met up with Nonni. You kept his attention on you while Ásta hit him in the head with a rock. He fell into you and you shoved him into the mud pool."

Billy shook his head. "You're making up stories." But his tone wasn't strong. His demeanor now looked scared rather than defensive.

Now was the time to make up a good story. He hoped the Icelandic judicial system wouldn't throw the information out on a technicality.

"We have information we've been keeping from

the public. We know a car used the dirt road at the south end of the lake. We found where the vehicle stopped and two sets of prints exited. The prints went to the mud pool where the body was found and back to the car. We know that Ásta called in sick that day and after the two of you killed Nonni, you got drunk, or acted like you were drunk, at lunch and made sure you parked so the person where you were staying would remember when you were in the apartment." Hawke stopped, shot a peripheral glance at Böðvarsson who had his gaze on Billy.

"Forensics was able to find bits of DNA on Nonni's coat, under the mud. The heat baked it into the fabric." He nodded to Böðvarsson. "Want to get that swab kit?"

The detective stood and walked to the door. He talked to the officer outside and sat back down. This was all a bluff, but Hawke hoped like hell it worked.

"All I did was shove him off of me. I didn't mean for him to land in the mud pool." Billy pointed a finger at Hawke. "I didn't kill him. Ásta did. And she laughed. The bitch laughed like a crazy person."

"I don't understand. If you were brought to Iceland by Nonni and his father to work out a money settlement, why did you go along with Ásta killing him? You should have known once his father finds out you were in on his son's death, he'll press harder to make sure your father goes broke trying to sue." That was the part Hawke didn't understand when he'd pieced together that Ásta and Billy had to have killed Nonni.

"I don't care what happens to my father. He's a prick. Always has been. I thought it was funny that Nonni called him out. But I had to stick up for my father if I wanted to get any financial support from him. I hadn't told him about the deal I'd made with Nonni and his dad. I planned to take the money and get as far from my father as I could. Then Ásta said she could get me more money if I helped her. I didn't know she planned on killing Nonni. I thought she had some kind of blackmail scheme to get more money out of him. When she hit him I couldn't believe it. Then he fell in my arms and I shoved him." For the first time, Weston looked as if he really was sorry for the death of Nonni.

"Did Ásta mention why she'd killed him?" Hawke wasn't going to let up. Weston was talking and he needed all the information he could get.

"She said if he wasn't going to be loyal to her, she wasn't about to let anyone else have him. And she was getting paid to make sure he suffered for what he'd done." Weston shook his head. "I asked her what she meant and she just laughed and said, 'Only I know the truth.'"

"She knew that the person paying her had picked the wrong person, but Ásta was using that person's need for revenge to fulfill her wish to kill Nonni." Hawke faced Böðvarsson. "Do we have enough?"

"We do." Böðvarsson told Weston about the recording and signing. Hawke walked to the door and out into the hall as Ásta was being put in the other interview room. She smiled at him as if she hadn't killed someone she'd proclaimed to love. Getting her to acknowledge her guilt and serve up Rowena Albright was going to be harder than making Weston crack. He was only an accomplice, not the person who cold-heartedly hit Nonni with a rock and laughed.

Chapter Twenty-nine

Hawke sat in Böðvarsson's office. They had decided to come up with a plan of action to get Ásta to break.

The detective had all the information that they'd gathered about her whereabouts on Wednesday and the interview with her employer, the restaurant, and the person where Weston was staying.

"We still need someone to say she left in her car on Wednesday and have her say she went to work, where they said Billy picked her up." Hawke glanced at Böðvarsson. "Can you send an officer to her apartment complex to find that out?"

Böðvarsson picked up the phone.

Hawke texted Katrín. *Did Nonni tell your group where he planned to hike on Wednesday morning?*

Less than a minute later, she responded. *He said he planned to hike south of Kleifarvatn Lake.*

How familiar is Ásta with that area?

She grew up in Hafnarfjörður.
Thank you.

Böðvarsson had finished his calls.

"Where is Half-narf-jorer?" Hawke asked.

"What?"

Hawke showed him the word on his phone.

"Hafnarfjörður. It's not far from Lake Kleifarvatn."

"Katrín says that is where Ásta grew up. She would know the roads and area around the lake and the mud pools." Hawke had finally found something to help them get the confession out of Ásta. That and her need to let the world know she was smarter than Rowena Albright. He had a feeling the young woman had taken this murder on for revenge and to prove she was better than an almost royal person. That was the vibe he'd been getting from her since their first meeting. She wanted to prove to everyone she was smarter and more cunning.

"Should we wait for the officer's information about her car or go start talking to her?" Hawke asked.

"Let's let her sit in there a little longer until we have everything clearly lined out. I also contacted the British embassy asking them to be ready to negotiate a meeting between us and Dr. and Mrs. Albright."

"That's a good idea. I've not dealt with people from other countries or of their status." Hawke would give anything to be sitting in the Rusty Nail eating a burger and talking with Merrilee and Justine about anything but what he'd run into here. Or sitting in the Bergmál sipping a beer with Dani.

"Do you think she's going to ask for a lawyer?" Böðvarsson asked.

Hawke shook his head. "She thinks she's outsmarted all of us. I have a feeling she'll lie all the way into a jail cell."

Böðvarsson's phone rang. He answered and flipped a paper from the file over and started writing. When he hung up, he had a smile on his face. "Two of Ásta's neighbors say they noticed her leave in her car at eight-thirty Wednesday morning. They remember because it was a work-day and she usually took the bus."

"That's good enough to catch her up in lies." Hawke stood. "Let's go have a talk."

They stepped in the room and as Hawke had figured, the young woman sat in the chair as if she were sitting in a bar, checking out the other patrons.

"Why did you ask me to come in here? Don't you have Nonni's killer?"

"Why would you think that?" Böðvarsson asked.

She glanced at him. "I had heard from someone, I don't remember who, that you'd caught the murderer."

"You know we haven't," Hawke said.

Her head whipped to face him. "What do you mean? How would I know if you have or haven't?"

He smiled. "Because we know you called in sick to work on Wednesday morning. Two of your neighbors remember you leaving in your car at eight-thirty."

"I wasn't feeling well. I went to the pharmacy for medicine." Her lips tipped into a smug smile.

"You went to Billy's, picked him up, and drove to Lake Kleifarvatn. Then you took a dirt road that put you close to the mud pool where Nonni died."

She smiled and shook her head. "That's not true. I went to the pharmacy and picked up medicine."

"If you were sick, why did you go to lunch with

Billy and get drunk?" Böðvarsson asked.

She swung her gaze his direction. "The medicine helped my headache."

"You and Billy had set it up to meet Nonni at the mud pool. We have the emails between him and Billy— the only person he was expecting. While Billy approached him from the front, you walked up behind and bashed your friend, the young man Einar said was going to marry you, in the back of the head with a rock." He tilted his head and glanced at Böðvarsson. "We have Nonni's hair and blood on the rock you used." He returned his gaze to Ásta. The smug smile remained pasted to her face. However, he could tell behind the blank stare, she was thinking. "We also have one hair, which must have fallen off your head, coat, or was maybe on the gloves you wore, that wasn't his. I'm guessing once we get a DNA swab from you, we'll have a match."

Böðvarsson did as before. He stood, went to the door, talked to the officer and returned.

Ásta watched him closely and tilted her head to listen to what he said. "We were never out there and you can't make me take a DNA test."

Hawke opened his hands palm up. "If you have nothing to hide you shouldn't care about a DNA test."

She shrugged. "I guess not. But I didn't kill him."

"You're right. You didn't kill him. You incapacitated him and left him to drown in a boiling mud pool." Hawke peered into her eyes. He saw no remorse. No compassion. If they hadn't caught her for this killing, she would have gone on committing more.

"We can drop the charge to assault instead of attempted murder, if you tell us why you and Billy wanted him dead." Hawke decided to play to her ego, rather than fear. She had no fear.

"We didn't want him dead. I wanted him to suffer the way he'd made me suffer." She played with the cuff of the sleeve of her shirt. "Billy wanted money. I discovered a way for us to both get what we wanted."

"What way?" Hawke leaned back as if what she was about to say was the least interesting thing to him. He'd learned enough about her to know she would use all her wits to make Rowena Albright out as the only villain in this scenario.

"Tuesday night, I went to Harpa to meet Nonni before everyone else arrived. I was standing by a woman when Riku walked up and hugged Nonni." Her eyes darkened with anger. "I could tell they felt more for one another than he'd ever felt for me. I said something and a woman overheard me. She asked why I was mad. I pointed out Nonni, and said, he couldn't keep his hands off girls. She asked me how I knew him. We went down to Bergmál and visited over drinks. She hated Nonni and wanted to set someone up to kill him. She asked me all about his habits, where he liked to go, and gave me her phone number." She tapped her fingers on the top of the table. "I'm thirsty." She peered at Böðvarsson. "Maybe they can bring some water when they bring the DNA test?" She raised an eyebrow.

It was as if she knew they'd made up the DNA fact.

The detective rose, walked to the door, and conversed with the officer. He sat back down at the table. "They are both coming. It's a busy day." He glanced at Hawke.

"Did you call this person when you discovered

where Nonni was hiking the following morning? Because you all sat there while he and I discussed the area he would hike." Hawke remained relaxed against the back of the chair. He didn't want this woman to know how badly he wanted her to reveal Mrs. Albright's, or her own, premeditation in killing Nonni.

She laughed. "Of course, I didn't tell her exactly where he was going. I wanted to get there first. They could work for their revenge. I just told her he was going to be the person your workshop tracked." She licked her lips. "What she did with the information was up to her."

"What did you get for the information? Billy said you offered to pay him more than Nonni planned to pay him." He decided to let her know that Billy had spilled everything. See if that rattled her.

"Billy told you I offered him money?" She laughed. "He about wet his pants when Nonni fell into him. He's the one who shoved Nonni into the mud pool and ran like a *hrætt barn*."

"Scared baby," Böðvarsson translated.

Ásta's eyes glistened with excitement. "He's the one who killed Nonni. How was I to pull him out?"

"You could have called for help," Hawke stated.

She shook her head. "There's limited reception. If anyone should be arrested for the murder, it's Billy." Ásta nodded her head solemnly.

The young woman was not only a keen manipulator, she was a good actress as well.

"Did the woman pay you for killing Nonni?" Hawke asked.

"I refused the money. I didn't kill him. I told her to pay Billy." She began fingering the cuff of her shirt, again.

Billy hadn't said a thing about receiving any money. Hawke had a feeling Ásta had decided she'd get more as blackmail than for the killing.

"Did she and Billy meet?" Böðvarsson asked. It appeared he was as anxious to get Rowena connected to the murder as Hawke.

"I wouldn't know. Billy said he didn't want anything to do with me afterwards. I gave her his phone number, but what the two of them did or didn't do, I have no idea."

The door opened. A female officer entered. She placed a glass of water on the table and opened a DNA swab test kit. She said something in Icelandic and Ásta opened her mouth. The swab was rubbed around inside her mouth and the officer left the room with the sample.

Ásta picked up the glass of water and drank it down to half. "Any more questions? I'd like to catch up to my friends. We're bar hopping tonight."

Böðvarsson glanced at Hawke. "I'm sorry but your statement is enough for us to arrest you for assault and not reporting a murder."

"I volunteered what I knew. I didn't kill Nonni." Ásta's face grew redder as she glared at each of them.

"You struck him on the head with a rock and allowed Billy to push him into a boiling mud pot. Then you did nothing about it." Hawke stood. "You will stand trial for that, if not for the murder of Jón Nonni Einarsson."

The young woman started screaming and shoved her body and chair back from the table. "How dare you call me a murderer. I didn't kill him. Billy did."

The officer outside the door and the female officer

who had swabbed Ásta's mouth, burst into the room. They handcuffed her and led her from the room. Böðvarsson turned off the recorder then.

Hawke stared at the empty chair. "We need to talk to Billy again. And let him see how she threw him under the bus."

Böðvarsson stared at him. "Under the bus?"

"It's a term meaning she is trying to put the whole murder on Billy. She knew where to go, she hit Nonni on the head. I have no doubt if Billy hadn't reacted like he did and the body hadn't ended up in the mud pool, she would have found a way to get Nonni in it."

"That I agree on. She is a sick young woman. I hope we can keep her in jail longer than for an assault." Böðvarsson glanced at his watch. "It is past the evening meal. Do you wish to get something to eat?"

"No. Let's get Billy in here and get this cleared up. I wish Ásta would have mentioned Rowena Albright. She's keeping that to herself to blackmail the woman."

"I agree. But if she did give Billy's number to Mrs. Albright, we should be able to get her side of things." Böðvarsson went to the door of the interview room and called out into the hall.

Five minutes later, a package of cookies and two coffees were brought to the room, and ten minutes later, Billy was escorted into the room.

His facial expression went blank when his gaze landed on them.

"Billy, we just finished talking to Ásta. She is saying you killed Nonni." Hawke picked up his cup of coffee and sipped. The brown liquid had the punch of a triple espresso.

The young man shook his head. "It was all her

idea. I thought we were just going to talk to him about money to stop the suit against him and his father. She hit him with the rock. You could tell she'd planned it all along. I wondered why she said, I should go talk to Nonni by myself and then she showed up behind him with that rock. I was just a distraction so she could hit him."

"She admits she hit him. But that you threw him in the mud pool. By the way, the mud pool is what killed him. He drowned." Hawke felt sympathetic to the man even though he had come to Iceland to betray his father and get money to start over. He'd also been duped by the young woman.

"It was just a reflex. When he fell toward me, I just shoved him away. I didn't know he'd go in the mud."

Böðvarsson pulled a small recorder out of his pocket. He set it on the table and clicked a button.

Chapter Thirty

Ásta's laugh rang through the room. "Of course, I didn't tell her exactly where he was going. I wanted to get there first. They could work for their revenge. I just told her he was going to be the person your workshop tracked." A pause. "What she did with the information was up to her."

"What did you get for the information? Billy said you offered to pay him more than Nonni planned to pay him." Hawke's voice.

He watched Billy's reaction to the recording. The young man's face grew red and his eyes narrowed.

"Billy told you I offered him money?" Ásta laughed again. "He about wet his pants when Nonni fell into him. He's the one who shoved Nonni into the mud pool and ran like a *hrætt barn*."

"Scared baby," Böðvarsson's voice.

"He's the one who killed Nonni. How was I to pull him out?"

"You could have called for help," Hawke stated.

"There's limited reception. If anyone should be arrested for the murder, it's Billy." Ásta's voice was firm.

Billy shot out of the chair. "She was the one who hit him. She went there to kill him. I only went to get money!" Anger had reddened his face and his lips twisted in a grimace.

The recording kept rolling.

"Did the woman pay you for killing Nonni?" Hawke asked.

"I refused the money. I didn't kill him. I told her to pay Billy." Ásta's voice.

Böðvarsson turned the recording off. "Did a woman contact you to pay you for Nonni's death?"

Billy shook his head. "No. Ásta told me she'd get the money from the woman and pay me." He wiped his hands across his face. "I didn't want money for Nonni's death." Billy's gaze hovered over each one of their faces. "I just want to go home and forget this all happened."

"That's not going to happen. You'll have to face charges of accessory to murder," Böðvarsson said, motioning for the young man to sit.

Hawke shifted to face the detective. "What if he helps us catch both women?"

Böðvarsson stared at Hawke. "What are you talking about?"

"We know who Ásta was talking about. What if we have Billy call her and set up a meet for her to pay him?"

Böðvarsson didn't look convinced.

Billy's face was losing color. "I don't know if I—"

Hawke cut him off. "I don't think he could get Ásta to admit to killing Nonni, but I know someone else who could."

"I can't okay any of this. I'll have to run it by the police commissioner and the prosecutor. And I already had Ásta booked. How are you going to get a confession out of her when she's in custody?" Böðvarsson glanced at Billy. "We can't talk about this with a suspect in the room."

Hawke glanced at his watch. 10:00. "Run it by whoever it needs to be run by and let me know in the morning what they say."

He wasn't sure if Böðvarsson could get his superiors to listen, but he would leave it up to the Icelandic Police to make the decision. He was going to go see a friendly face.

Dani was still up when he arrived at his room at the Center Hotel.

"Is everything solved?" she asked, sitting in a chair, wearing a loose-fitting pair of pajamas and looking at a map of Iceland.

"Yes, and no. We know who killed the young man physically, but we still need to find a way to pin it on the woman who wanted him dead." Hawke started to fill a glass with water.

"There's beer in the fridge," Dani pointed to the small refrigerator, he'd thought about stocking all week but hadn't had the time.

"Thanks." He grabbed a bottle, opened it and sat in the chair beside her. "How was your trip today?"

She set the map down and peered into his eyes. "It was beautiful. I wish you could have been with me.

Will you be able to see sights with me tomorrow?"

He sighed. "It will depend on the answers Detective Inspector Böðvarsson can get from his superiors tonight."

"I see. Should I plan on keeping this room a couple more days and do day trips out of here?" She didn't sound upset. That was what he liked about her. She understood his profession came first.

"That would probably be the best. And I'd like to go to the funeral for the victim later in the week." He sipped his beer and studied her.

Dani peered into his eyes. "Tell me about him."

Hawke spent half an hour telling her about meeting Nonni and what he'd learned about the young man since his death.

"He sounds like a young man who would have made a difference in the world, had he been allowed to live." Dani summed up in one sentence the way Hawke felt.

Wednesday morning Hawke woke to his phone buzzing. Dani was snuggled up against his side. He reached over her to get to the phone.

Böðvarsson.

"Hello?" he answered, his voice still scratchy from sleep.

"Did I wake you?" The question was more of a jest than a question.

"Yeah. Did you get a go ahead with our plan?" Hawke sat up, scrubbing his free hand up and down his face.

"The Police Commissioner and the Prosecutor will be in my office in an hour. They both wish to speak with you."

"Great. Have coffee and pastries ready." He hung up and slid his legs over the edge of the bed.

"You're leaving already?" Dani asked, not moving from where she was snuggled under the covers.

"Yeah. If all goes well, I'll be done with this by noon. Don't stray too far." He leaned over, kissed the top of her head, and hurried into the shower.

Böðvarsson waited for Hawke at the entrance to the police station. "The commissioner and prosecutor aren't very happy I'm advocating for *grípa til örþrifaráða* from an American."

Hawke studied him. "What does that mean?"

"Basically, we would resort to extreme measures as these to put innocent people in danger and all of our jobs in jeopardy by trying to get a nearly royal to prove she wanted someone dead and the person who killed our victim to confess to someone not in law enforcement." Böðvarsson opened the police station door.

"That sums it up. We can have wires on Billy and Riku and we'll be close enough to arrest once they each say or do what we need to know." Hawke slapped Böðvarsson on the back. "It's easy."

The detective opened one of the interview rooms. Two men, one of large stature and one average, stood in a corner talking. They both faced the door and their gazes took in Hawke.

He stepped forward extending his hand. "Commissioner." The larger of the two put his hand out and Hawke shook. "Prosecutor." He shook the other man's hand. "Thank you both for taking time to come down and listen to our proposal."

The two moved to chairs across the table from Hawke and Böðvarsson.

"What you are proposing could discredit not only our police but our country," the commissioner said.

"I realize we are dealing with a woman of importance. But I also feel tricking her is the only way to get her to admit to what she did. The younger woman in the equation would have killed the victim at some time, but the older woman's desire for his death gave the murderer the shove she needed to commit it sooner."

"I have read all the subterfuge Mrs. Albright had Ms. Tumaini do to make her look like the murderer, I don't see how, even if she pays this Billy Weston, we can bring charges against her," the prosecutor said. "For all we know, Mrs. Albright believes that Ms. Tumaini killed the victim. And that Ms. Tumaini will be charged."

Hawke raised a hand. "If that's how you think, then we'll have Ms. Tumaini go to Mrs. Albright, with a wire, and tell her she didn't kill the victim and the police know it was a for hire killing, and they have the person responsible who is telling everything. That will take her to the young woman who really did it."

"Ásta is in jail." Böðvarsson said.

"We need to let her out long enough for Mrs. Albright to contact her, and as we are gathering the two, have Riku confront the young woman." Hawke nodded to all three men at the table. "That's the best way to clear it all up and get the truth. I don't think Billy Weston could carry out what we need done, anyway." He glanced at Böðvarsson. "We need to tell Kanika what she needs to do. She can either go to Mrs. Albright or call her on the phone. I think the phone would be more convincing."

Böðvarsson nodded.

"We haven't said yes to any of this," the commissioner interrupted.

Hawke nodded and gave the man his full attention. "I'm not trying to tell you what to do, but given this is such a unique situation, I think a unique move on the law enforcement's part is the way to go. Otherwise, you'll have a murderer get off for attempted murder or assault, while a young man who shoved the falling body off him out of fear will go to jail for murder. And a woman who set someone else up to go down for the murder and agreed to pay someone to kill the victim, will walk away without so much as a slap on the hand." He glanced around the table. "That isn't justice to me. Is it to you?"

The three began a discussion in Icelandic while Hawke tried to read their faces. The two stood and walked out of the room. He shifted his attention to Böðvarsson. "Well?"

"The commissioner is on the fence, but the prosecutor wants us to do it. Let's go see Kanika." Böðvarsson stood and walked to the door.

"What about letting Ásta loose?"

"I'll call and have that happen while Kanika is making her call. If Ásta wants to get out of here, she'll need money and could contact Mrs. Albright. I'll also put a tail on Mrs. Albright and on Ásta so we know where they both are at all times."

"While you set all of that up, I'll let Riku know we'll need her assistance.

Chapter Thirty-one

Riku sat in the back seat of Böðvarsson's car. Hawke was in the passenger seat. The police watching Mrs. Albright said she'd remained in the hotel apartment, but her husband had left thirty minutes earlier, after Ásta had been seen making a phone call.

"What if they only meet in the hotel room?" Riku asked. "How do I come upon Ásta?"

"You'll wait in the hotel lobby after Ásta goes to see Mrs. Albright. When she comes down, you confront her about Nonni." Hawke had been playing all kinds of scenarios through his mind. It was best to have Riku in a public place given Ásta's rage and hatred.

"That is good plan." Riku leaned back in the seat.

Böðvarsson had a listening device in his ear. "Ásta just drove up to the hotel."

Hawke put his hand on the door handle.

"She's in."

"How do we hear what they say?" Riku asked.

"We don't. The flowers were changed out with fresh ones and a listening device." Böðvarsson grimaced. "We can't use this against either one of them in court, but we might be able to get one of them to confess to the conversation or the whole plot by having them recorded."

"She just knocked on the suite and was let in." Böðvarsson pointed to the door.

Hawke and Riku exited the car and walked to the hotel. Motion on the third floor caught his eye. Glancing up, he noticed that the two women stood out on the deck. He hoped there had been fresh flowers put out there or they would have nothing.

Inside the lobby, he led Riku to a chair. "Wait here. When you see her, approach, don't let her out the door, and accuse her of ruining what you and Nonni had with her jealousy. I'll be watching where she can't see me. You'll be safe."

"I know. I hope she will say what you need." Riku folded her hands and placed them in her lap.

"Me, too," Hawke said, walking to a pillar and slipping around the side, where he could see Riku and keep an eye on the elevator.

They didn't have long to wait. The elevator doors opened. Ásta stepped out with a smug smirk on her face. Until Riku stood and walked toward her.

"How did you find me here?" Ásta accused.

"I am waiting for my father. He is visiting. What are you doing here?" Riku stepped in front of the other woman when she tried to step around her.

"Seeing a friend. Out of my way." Ásta put an arm out to push Riku to the side.

"You are not going anywhere until you tell me why

you took Nonni away from me." Riku swung her arms in what looked like a martial arts move to push Ásta's arm away.

"I didn't take Nonni from you. You took him from me. We were talking about spending our lives together until you showed up here two years ago. After that, all he talked about was Riku this and Riku that." She sneered. "But he slept with me when you weren't around."

"He told me, he used you." Riku's face was blank. Hawke couldn't tell if she knew about Nonni sleeping with Ásta and didn't care because of what Nonni said, or if she was tamping down her disappointment to get the other woman to mess up.

"Used me?" Ásta's voice rose. "I used him. He was so proud of how he helped people. How he kept us from using drugs." She laughed. "I was using and he didn't even know."

"How could you lie to him? He was honest, loyal, and kind." Riku's face hardened. "All the things you aren't. I am glad he is dead and does not have to learn how terrible you are."

Ásta laughed. "You loved him, didn't you?"

Tears trickled down Riku's face. "Yes. With all my heart. And he loved me. We were to speak of marriage."

"I should have waited. Then you would have been a widow." Ásta started to go around Riku.

The young woman's arm was a blur as she grabbed Ásta by the arm and jerked her back around. "You killed him, didn't you?"

"Let go of me!" Ásta said in a growl between clenched teeth.

"Not until you tell me the truth. Were you the cause of his death?" Riku twisted Ásta's arm.

"Let go of me. Yes, I hit him on the head with a rock and if Billy hadn't shoved him in the boiling mud, I would have. He was going to leave me for you. You!"

Riku shoved Ásta to the ground and walked back to the chair where she sat down. Tears ran down her cheeks.

Hawke strode over, picked Ásta up off the ground, and handcuffed her.

She started yelling in Icelandic. Hawke didn't have any idea what she was saying but several of the hotel staff came hurrying over.

Böðvarsson came through the doors, shouting something, and everyone backed off.

Once the detective and a woman dressed in a maid's uniform took control of Ásta, Hawke walked over to Riku. He knelt beside the chair. "I'm sorry you had to hear the gory details of how Nonni died. You know she said that to hurt you, just like she killed Nonni to hurt you."

"Yes. But it hurts that he believed she was a friend and she did so much to harm him."

"I agree. Do you want me to call your father to come get you or do you want to ride back to the police station with us?" Hawke held out a hand to help her stand.

"I wish to see her being punished for what she has done." Riku shoved the tears off her face and peered at him.

"You won't see that until the trial. How about I walk you back to your hotel. I think we could both use the fresh air and sunshine that is out today."

She agreed.

Böðvarsson was waiting for them by his car.

"We're going to walk back to the Marina Hotel. I'll catch up with you later. You have the recording. But what about Mrs. Albright?" Hawke asked.

Böðvarsson grinned. "They were on the deck. I had someone stationed to take photos. And we have the confrontation and her paying Ásta, who we now have proof killed Nonni." He patted Riku. "Good job. Everything will come to both women as it should."

"That's all we wanted." Hawke put an arm around Riku's shoulders. "Let's enjoy our walk."

"We finally meet," Böðvarsson walked toward Hawke and Dani at Nonni's funeral.

Hawke put a hand on Dani's back, making her take one step forward. "Dani Singer, this is Detective Inspector Böðvarsson who I worked with to find Nonni's killer."

"Please, I am Ari. I am happy to meet you." Böðvarsson's eyes twinkled. "I expected to see you in overalls."

Dani frowned at Hawke.

He chuckled. "Ari tried to get me to buy you a dress that you'd never wear. I told him you liked jeans and overalls."

"I see. Did Hawke tell you I'm a pilot? I feel more comfortable in jumpsuits and overalls." Dani hooked her arm with Ari's. "We have two more days before we leave your country. What do you think is a good place for us to see?"

Böðvarsson glanced over his shoulder and winked at Hawke. Dani was as tight-lipped as himself. He didn't need to worry she'd answer any personal questions the detective asked her.

"Mr. Hawke."

He spun around and faced Mr. Tanaka and Riku. "Hello."

"We wish to thank you for not giving up on the truth about Nonni's death," Mr. Tanaka said.

"I think our cultures are alike. My ancestors mourned the dead even though they were being cradled in the Creator's arms. It is the loss of their time on earth with the ones they love that leave us grieving the most."

"He lived too few years for the depth of his compassion for others." A tear glistened in the man's eye.

Riku hugged Hawke. "Thank you, Mr. Hawke. Because of you, we all know the truth." Her face turned to the left.

Hawke followed her gaze and found Bragi. He finally knew the truth about Wanza. Hawke wondered which was better. That he knew she died but had wanted to be with him or if he'd gone on thinking she'd found someone else?

"The truth is always the best." Hawke released Riku and went in search of Dani and Böðvarsson. He'd had enough mourning, he wanted to see more of Iceland and return home. On the way home, he would set up a time Dani could go meet his mom.

Thank you for reading book five in the Gabriel Hawke Novels. I enjoyed taking Hawke to another country and out of his element. I'm anxious to get started on his next adventure back in Wallowa County. That book is a result of an investigation that actually happened. I'll put my spin on it.

Leaving a review is the best way to show your appreciation to an author for entertaining you. All you have to do is leave a brief sentence or two about why you liked the book or what about the book interested you and a star rating. That's it!

While you're waiting for the next Hawke book, check out my Shandra Higheagle Mystery series.

Paty

Continue investigating and tracking with Hawke as his series continues. If you missed his other books they are:

Murder of Ravens
Book 1
Print ISBN 978-1-947983-82-3

Mouse Trail Ends
Book 2
Print ISBN 978-1-947983-96-0

Rattlesnake Brother
Book 3
Print ISBN 978-1-950387-06-9

Chattering Blue Jay
Book 4
Print ISBN 978-1-950387-64-9

About the Author

Paty Jager grew up in Wallowa County and has always been amazed by its beauty, history, and ruralness. After doing a ride-along with a Fish and Wildlife State Trooper in Wallowa County, she knew this was where she had to set the Gabriel Hawke series.

Paty is an award-winning author of 45 novels of murder mystery and western romance. All her work has Western or Native American elements in them along with hints of humor and engaging characters. She and her husband raise alfalfa hay in rural eastern Oregon. Riding horses and battling rattlesnakes, she not only writes the western lifestyle, she lives it.

By following her at one of these places you will always know when the next book is releasing and if she has any sales or giveaways:
Website: http://www.patyjager.net
Blog: https://writingintothesunset.net/
FB Page: https://www.facebook.com/PatyJagerAuthor/
Pinterest: https://www.pinterest.com/patyjag/
Twitter: https://twitter.com/patyjag
Goodreads:
http://www.goodreads.com/author/show/1005334.Paty_Jager
Newsletter- Mystery: https://bit.ly/2IhmWcm
Bookbub - https://www.bookbub.com/authors/paty-jager

Windtree
Press

Thank you for purchasing this Windtree Press
publication. For other books of the heart, please visit
our website at www.windtreepress.com.

For questions or more information contact us
at info@windtreepress.com.

Windtree Press
www.windtreepress.com

Hillsboro, OR 971